MIDDLE SCHOOL
GET ME OUT OF HERE!

MIDDLE SCHOOL
GET ME OUT OF HERE!

James Patterson

AND CHRIS TEBBETTS

ILLUSTRATED BY LAURA PARK

LITTLE, BROWN AND COMPANY
NEW YORK · BOSTON

Copyright © 2012 by James Patterson
Illustrations by Laura Park

Little, Brown and Company

Hachette Book Group
237 Park Avenue, New York, NY 10017
Visit our website at www.lb-kids.com

Little, Brown and Company is a division of Hachette Book Group, Inc.
The Little, Brown name and logo are trademarks of Hachette Book Group, Inc.

The publisher is not responsible for websites (or their content) that are not owned by the publisher.

First U.S. Edition published in May 2012 by Little, Brown and Company
First International Edition: May 2012

ISBN 978-0-316-20671-6 (hc) / 978-0-316-20966-3 (international)

10 9 8 7 6 5 4 3 2 1

RRD-H

Printed in the United States of America

THE AUTHORS WOULD LIKE TO THANK:

Andrew Junge at Oakland School for the Arts

Alice Trageser at Hinesburg Community School

Janie Bynum

Lisa Pagano

CHAPTER 1

WHOOM!

Well, who'd have thought so much could change in one summer? Not me, that's for sure. Not my best buddy, Leonardo the Silent.

Probably not the folks at Airbrook Arts Community School either. That's where I was supposed to start seventh grade in the fall.

Supposed to. You caught that, right? There's a reason my last book was called *Middle School, The Worst* Years *of My Life*. Sixth grade was only the start. I've got a whole lot more to tell you about. But first I should introduce myself.

Anyway, I guess I should have seen it coming. It's like every time things start to look okay in my crazy life, something always comes along to change it. It's like it just falls out of the sky.

And *everything* changed on the day Swifty's Diner burned to the ground.

Here's what happened. See, there's this thing called a grease trap over the grill at the diner, where Swifty (also known as Fred) cooked about fifteen dozen greasy burgers every day. If you don't clean out the trap once in a while, it turns into a giant fireball, just waiting to go off.

And guess what?

I didn't get to see much. I was in the storage room in the back, just passing the time and waiting for Mom to finish her lunch shift. Then all of a sudden, I heard this giant *WHOOM!* People started yelling, the fire alarm started blaring, and I could smell smoke.

Anybody smell smoke?

A second later, Mom was there.

"Come on, Rafe," she said. "We have to go—right now!" And she hustled me out the back door.

Nobody was hurt, but flames were coming through the windows and up through the roof before the Hills Village Fire Department even got there.

By the time the firefighters finally put out the fire, Swifty's Diner looked more like Swifty's Big Pile of Ashes. Everything was all black and smoking, and the restaurant was just—gone.

And that's not all.

No Swifty's meant no job for Mom.

No job meant no money to pay the rent on our house.

No house meant we had to pack up all our stuff and get out.

(See what I mean about everything changing?)

The only place we could go was Grandma Dotty's. She told Mom we could come stay there as long as we wanted, which was really nice of her and everything, but the problem was, she lived in the city, about eighty miles away. In other words, way too far for me to even think about going to Airbrook anymore. Now I was going to be starting seventh grade at some big-city middle school, where kids like me get turned into chopped meat every single day.

So there you have it. Chapter 1 isn't even over, and I'm already starting a whole new life. Try to keep up if you can. This is only the very beginning, where I say—

Good-bye, Hills Village!

Good-bye, lucky breaks!

And hello, seventh grade!

CHAPTER 2

MOVING DAY

H ere's what it looked like on the day we left Hills Village. Not too shabby, huh?

CHAPTER 3

OR SOMETHING LIKE THAT

Yeah, I wish.

If you know me, then you know I have what my mom likes to call an "active imagination" and what some of my teachers might call a "tendency to lie."

I like to think of it as putting my own spin on the things that happen to me. But don't worry—I'll always steer you straight. In fact, here's what it really looked like when we left town:

11

Those people waving are Ms. Donatello and Jeanne Galletta, two of the only people who were nice to me at Hills Village Middle School.

Ms. Donatello was my sixth-grade English teacher. I used to call her the Dragon Lady, but she turned out to be human after all. She was also the one who got me into Airbrook, before my big plans went down the garbage disposal.

As for Jeanne, she was nice to everyone, so I don't even know if that counts. When I told her I'd try to keep in touch, she said I could leave a message on her HVMS student page. Was that a good sign? You tell me. I don't exactly have a ton of experience with girls. Or friends. Much less... girlfriends. Still, if there was one person I was going to miss, it was Jeanne.

So if you haven't guessed by now, it's not like I was leaving behind some kind of perfect track record in Hills Village. Which is maybe the understatement of the year.

And if you want to know what I mean, just check out the next chapter.

CHAPTER 4

MY TOP TEN
(ACTUALLY ONLY SIX)

Rafe Khatchadorian's Top ~~Ten~~ Six Biggest Accomplishments From Sixth Grade (try not to be too impressed):

I GOT LOTS OF exercise.

#2

I CAME UP WITH SOME PRETTY COOL ART.

#3

I GOT TO RIDE IN A FAST CAR.

#4

I LEARNED TO PAINT.

15

This is going to be great," Mom kept saying while we drove into the city. "I can't wait to show you guys around. There's so much to do here, and you're going to love the park."

I stopped listening after a while. I think my sister, Georgia, did too. We both just stared out the window, trying to imagine living here.

Fill in whatever city you want—New York, Chicago, Boston, South Bend, Boise, Omaha... whatever. Just imagine lots of shiny skyscrapers, perfectly clean sidewalks, and millions of happy people catching money as it rains out of the sky.

Now think about the exact opposite of that. Got it?

Welcome to Grandma Dotty's neighborhood. Also known as our new home.

"This is where you grew up?" Georgia said, and not in a nice way.

"It used to be...different," Mom said, but you could tell she meant *better*. Now I knew why Grandma always came to visit us in Hills Village and not the other way around.

All the houses on the block were crammed together, one after the other. They didn't have any side yards or front yards. Just sidewalks. I saw a lot of garbage cans and graffiti too.

"I'm never going to make any friends here," Georgia whined.

"Come on, honey. I know it's a big adjustment, but you've got to stay positive," Mom said.

"Okay," Georgia said. "I'm *positive* I'm never going to make any friends here."

Mom took a deep breath. "How about you, Rafe? Are you ready to give city life a chance?"

"Sure," I said. "Why not?"

The truth was, I felt exactly the same way as Georgia. I didn't want to live here, and I *definitely* didn't want to go to school here.

But unlike my little sister, who never knows when to shut her mouth, I knew that Mom was doing the best she could.

"Well, here we are," she said, and stopped in front of the fifth house from the end of the block. "Six twenty-five Killarney Avenue."

Georgia made a sound like she was coughing up a hair ball. "It's the worst one on the street!" she said.

"It just needs some spiffing up," Mom said. "You'll see. All it takes is a little imagination. Isn't that right, Rafe?"

"Sure," I said. "Just a little imagination. That's all."

Hills Village
80 miles

CHAPTER 6

SMALL AND FULL

I always used to hear Mom say Grandma Dotty was a big pack rat. And to be honest, I never really thought about what that meant. I just thought:  But as soon as we walked into her house, I knew exactly what it meant. If there were two words to describe Grandma's place, they would be *small* and *full*.

"Come in, come in, come in!" she said, hugging us all like crazy. "Do you have much more to bring in from the car?" Grandma asked Mom.

"Not much," Mom said. Most of our stuff was in a big storage locker back in Hills Village.

"That's good. I'm a little short on closet space at the moment," Grandma said, but it looked to me like she was a little short on Rafe-Mom-and-Georgia space too.

"What's with the long faces, kiddos?" Grandma asked me and Georgia. "You two look like someone's dog just died."

"They're just tired," Mom told her. "It's been a big day."

"This little one's ready to drop," Grandma said, looking at Georgia. "And Ralph, I'll bet you could eat a horse and a half by now."

"Um…" I said, but I was thinking—

All of a sudden, I felt even weirder about being here.

"It's *Rafe*, Mom," my mom said. "Not Ralph."

"Well, of course it is," Grandma said. "I'm sorry, Rafe. Just a slip of the tongue. Now, come on—who's hungry?"

I looked at Mom, and she nodded like everything was going to be fine. And in fact, whatever Grandma was cooking smelled amazing, just like Mom's lasagna from home.

Then, when we came into the kitchen, I saw something else familiar.

"Isn't that one of yours?" I asked Mom.

"Sure is," she said.

The last time I'd seen any of her paintings on a wall was at Swifty's Diner, but those had gone up in smoke, along with everything else.

"In this house, your mother is a famous artist," Grandma said. Then she turned around and bowed right down in front of Mom.

Mom laughed. Georgia did too, for the first time in about a week.

"That's the ticket!" Grandma said. "Much better."

She reached over and tickled Georgia under the chin, and pretty soon everyone was laughing.

"Now *these* are the Khatchadorians I remember," Grandma said, and hugged me all over again. "We're going to have a great time together. Isn't that right, Ralph?"

CHAPTER 7

A NiGHT ON THe TOWN

It's two in the morning and I'm wide awake. Mom gave me the choice between sleeping on the couch downstairs and sharing the guest room with Georgia, which of course was no contest. At least down here I have a little privacy.

Still, I can't sleep. I'm too busy trying to figure out how I'm going to get through this year. It hasn't even started yet, and all I see is rough road ahead.

I finally drift off, but it isn't long before Leonardo the Silent strolls into my dreams.

"What are you doing?" he says.

"I'm trying to sleep," I tell him.

"No, you're trying to mope," Leo tells me. "Come on. There's a whole big city out there. We've got better things to do."

He's right, of course.

I jump out of bed (out of couch?), and we make a fake Rafe under the blankets, including a superrealistic mask of my face, just in case Mom or Grandma comes down in the middle of the night. Then we slip into our stealth gear and out the door. A second later we hit the streets.

"Where do you want to go first?" Leo asks.

"Somewhere up high," I say. "Let's get a look at what we're dealing with."

"Excellent choice." He points the way toward the city's tallest building. "Good thing I brought the climbing gear."

We move like shadows, using back alleys and hidden passages to get there. With all the shortcuts Leo knows, we're standing at the base of Megamega Towers in no time.

"So that's what three hundred stories looks like," I say.

"Wait till you see it from the top," Leo tells me.

As soon as we're harnessed up, we step into our suction-cup boots and head toward the sky.

"Don't look down until we get there," Leo tells me. "It'll be worth the wait."

He's right about that too. Once we hit the roof
of that skyscraper, I can see for miles and miles in
every direction.

"Can't do this in Hills Village," Leo says.

The cars below look like baby ants with tiny
headlights, and the whole city is spread out in front
of me like the world's biggest game board. All I
have to do now is pick my next move.

"Maybe this year isn't going to be so bad after all," I say.

"Well, if you like this," Leo says, "you're going to love the ride down."

As we step into our portable hang glider, the sun just starts to show over the horizon. My first night in the big city has flown by already. Mom will be waking up soon, and I've got to head back.

But in the meantime—what a view!

CHAPTER 8

TiMe OUT

Okay, time out for a second.

If you read the last book, then you already know all about Leo. I mean, especially the part about how he's not really real. But if that's news to you, then there's some other stuff you should probably know too. It's kind of heavy, but let me get it out of the way now.

The real Leonardo was my twin brother. He got sick and died when we were both three years old. It was really sad, for sure, but it was also a long time ago. I barely remember any of it.

The point is, I've always wondered what Leo would be like if he were still around. I guess that's who I've been talking to all this time—like an *idea* of Leo, also known as Leonardo the Silent.

So now, if you're thinking—

CUCKOO CUCKOO CUCKOO!

—all I can tell you is, I'm not. Seriously. I'm just…well, I don't really know what I am. Imaginative, I guess. A loner, for sure. But not cuckoo.

Mom says Leo's my muse. That's someone who helps an artist get ideas and think things through, even though the muse isn't really there. And, yeah, that pretty much describes him. Leo may not be real, but in some weird way he helps me deal with the things that are. That's also why he's my best friend.

Hey, I never said it wasn't complicated. I just said I'm not crazy.

CHAPTER 9

MOM THROWS A CURVEBALL

The next morning, Mom made really good French toast for breakfast. It's Georgia's favorite, with bananas and maple syrup. And extra cinnamon on mine.

"Rafe, when you're done, I want you to put on the shirt I left out for you," Mom said. "And clean pants, please."

That stopped me with a mouthful of everything. Nothing good ever happens in clothes your mom picks out for you.

"What's going on?" I said.

She just smiled and slid me some seconds. "It's a surprise," she said.

"Where's Rafe going?" Georgia said. "What's happening? Can I come?"

"Everyone's coming," Mom said, but that's all she would tell. A little while later, we were piled into the car and headed up Killarney Avenue.

Mom really knew her way around the city. She pointed out the science museum, the IMAX, the ballpark, and a whole bunch of other stuff. I knew she was trying to get us excited about living here.

What I didn't understand was why my shirt had to be tucked in right now.

Finally, I said, "Mom—please. Just tell me where we're going."

"Okay, okay. We're almost there anyway," she said. "Now, don't be nervous—"

1 FIRST PRIZE
"What NOT to Say to Your Kid"

"Don't Be Nervous"

2

"Just Eat It"

3

"Because I Said So"

"What do you mean?" I said. "Why shouldn't I be nervous?"

"Well, I know how disappointed you were about not going to Airbrook," Mom said. "But this morning, we might be able to do something about that. You've got an interview, Rafe. At Cathedral School of the Arts."

I don't know what I was expecting her to say, but that wasn't it. I kind of thought Airbrook was a one-time opportunity.

"You mean there's more than one of these places?" I said.

"Cathedral's even better," Mom said. "It's a public school, so it's free. But you do have to be admitted. That's what the interview is for."

And that's when I realized what she meant about being nervous.

I hadn't even seen this Cathedral place yet, and I already knew I wanted to go there. If it was anything like I was imagining, it could be the greatest school on Earth.

"I don't get it," I said. "How did this even happen?"

"Actually, it wasn't me who got you the interview," Mom said.

I looked over at Grandma.

"Don't look at me, Ralphie," she said. "I'm as confused as you are."

"It was Ms. Donatello," Mom said, and my head snapped back to her like I was watching tennis.

"Wha-huh?"

"In fact"—Mom pointed across the street from where we'd just parked—"there she is right now."

CHAPTER 10

THE RETURN OF
THE DRAGON LADY

When we got out of the car, Ms. Donatello was waiting for us on the sidewalk. She had a big smile on her face and an even bigger black leather folder under her arm.

"I'll bet you didn't expect to see me again so soon, did you?" she said.

I didn't expect to see her again at all, but I didn't say that.

"Here." She gave me the big folder. "I brought a portfolio of your artwork from last year. Now come on—we don't want to be late!"

We followed Ms. D. through the front door and up to the main office, where the interview was supposed to happen.

On the outside, Cathedral was just some regular building, but it was pretty cool on the inside, with lots of big windows, and stairs going in all different directions. Ms. D. told us it used to be a brick factory about a hundred years ago, and Mom said things like *oh my*, and *how wonderful*.

Meanwhile, I was bringing up the rear and freaking out while nobody noticed. This was starting to look like a suicide mission. There were paintings and drawings all over the place, and as far as I could tell, every kid who went to this school was a way better artist than me.

"Maybe we shouldn't have come," I said.

Everyone looked at me. Even Georgia.

"Rafe, you're going to do fine," Ms. Donatello said.

I looked at the office door. "What's going to happen in there?"

"First, they'll take a look at your portfolio..."

"…and then ask a few questions about some of your drawings."

"After that, you'll be asked to leave the room, and they'll take some time to consider your application."

And before I even know it's happened, I'm at the point of no return. The door to the office is already swinging open. They're waiting for me inside.

"Anything else I should know?" I ask Ms. D.

Except, Ms. D. isn't Ms. D. anymore. Her eyes have re-formed into yellow slits, and her breath has turned to smoke. She paws at the big black folder I'm holding. "Everything you need is right in there," she says.

When I look, I see that she's hidden my old sword inside the portfolio. Amazing! The Dragon Lady, once my enemy, is now my ally.

But she's also taken me as far as she can go. Whatever's waiting on the other side of that door, I'm going to have to face it alone. The only question now is whether I'll be coming back alive...

...or not.

CHAPTER 11

THE INTERVIEW

The inside of the interrogation room is cold. I can see my breath in the air, but none of the three strangers sitting across from me seem to notice.

They all look human enough, but I know better. It's a careful disguise, meant to make me feel comfortable, so I'll drop my guard.

"Khatchadorian, is it?" says the tall one in the middle. He smiles and beckons me closer.

"That's right," I say. "Rafe."

"Ms. Donatello tells us you were named for Rafael Sanzio, the great painter. Are you a fan of his work?"

I play along, for now. "Sure," I say, but I keep my eyes moving around the room. There could be hidden traps anywhere, just waiting to spring.

"Well, let's see what you've brought with you," another one says. I can see the warts just under her fake human skin as she puts out a hand to take my portfolio.

This is it. If I'm going to make my move, now's the time. I reach inside—and my sword comes out in a flash.

Chairs go tumbling. Skins fly off. Claws extend. In less than two seconds, I'm facing down the ugliest set of triplets you've ever seen. They stretch into their new bodies and bare their fangs. One of them lets out a long, angry growl.

No. Not angry, I realize. *Hungry*. That was someone's stomach.

Then all at once, they attack. I keep my head down and follow my instincts.

I swing!

I weave!

I dodge!

A trapdoor opens under my feet, and I jump out of the way just in time.

I thrust!

I thrust again!

And again!

So far I'm holding my own, but I don't know how long I'm going to be able to keep this up. Meanwhile, they keep coming—one at a time, and then all together, screaming to each other in their secret language.

I lose a little ground and back up. Lose a little more ground and back up some more.

Then, before I even know it's happened, I'm cornered. Exactly where I don't want to be. They've got me on all sides now.

I keep my sword raised, waiting for them to close in. But instead they hold their ground—and it doesn't take long to figure out why.

The walls behind me start to rumble. I hear the ceiling crack overhead. It's another trap!

By the time I look up, it's too late. All I see now is a shower of boulders headed my way as the whole place caves in around me.

That's it.

I had my chance and I blew it.

This interview is over.

CHAPTER 12

IN

"I'm sure it wasn't as bad as you think," Mom said afterward.

"It was worse," I told her. "Even *I* wouldn't let me into this school."

It's like the whole Cathedral interview was just a blur. I showed them my portfolio and gave a bunch of dumb answers to their questions, but I couldn't even tell you what I said.

Now we were stuck out in the hall again, waiting for them to come out and give me the bad news.

"Don't worry, kiddo. If they don't want you, it's their loss," Grandma said.

"Why don't we just wait and see what they say?" Ms. Donatello told me.

"I have to go to the bathroom," Georgia said.

I didn't want to talk anymore, so I just made like Leonardo the Silent and kept my mouth shut after that.

Finally, the office door opened, and Mr. Crawley, the director of the school, came over to talk to us. I tried not to look like I wanted to disappear. Or self-destruct. Or both.

"First of all, Rafe," he said, "you should know there are three things we look for in an applicant. One of those is experience. A lot of the students at Cathedral have been studying art since before they could write."

"Sure," I said. "I get it. No problem."

But he wasn't done yet.

"The other two things we look for are talent and persistence," he said. "Not only is that portfolio of yours full of artistic promise, it's also just *full*. When I see that, I see a boy who would probably keep drawing whether anyone was paying attention or not."

I looked at Mom, trying to see if she was happy. I still couldn't tell if this was good news or bad news yet.

"All of which is to say—"

Mr. Crawley put out his hand for me to shake, and I felt like everything was moving in slow motion.

"—we've approved your application."

I couldn't believe it. Like maybe it was a joke, or they had the wrong Rafe or something.

"Are you serious?" I said.

"Serious as Picasso's Blue Period," Mr. Crawley said, and Mom and Ms. D. cracked up while I shook his hand. "Welcome to Cathedral!"

And even though it still didn't feel real, I'll tell you what else. Those were the three best words I'd heard in a long, long time.

GREETINGS FROM THE BIG CITY!

Back at Grandma's place, I got up my nerve to do something absolutely terrifying: I wrote a note to a girl.

To: JGinHV@hvms.edu
From: Rafemonster@gogomail.com
Subject: You're never going to believe this

Hey, Jeanne,

How's it going over there in bad old Hills Village? Anyone miss me yet? (Anyone even notice I'm gone? ☺)

You'll never believe how things are going here. On a scale of one to ten, I'd give it about a fourteen, because guess who just got into Cathedral School of the Arts? (I'll give you a hint. It starts with an *R* and ends with an *AFE*.)

Are you still there? Or did you just die of shock? I was pretty surprised too, but I won't tell them they made a mistake if you won't, ha-ha. School starts on Monday, so wish me luck because I think I'm going to need all I can get.

And write back if you want. (No pressure.)

Rafe

CHAPTER 14

TWENTY-TWO HOURS AND FORTY-NINE MINUTES LATER (NOT THAT I WAS COUNTING OR ANYTHING)

To: Rafemonster@gogomail.com
From: JGinHV@hvms.edu
Subject: Re: You're never going to believe this

Hi, Rafe—
That's great. Congratulations!
—JG

CHAPTER 15

THE FIRST DAY OF THE REST OF MY LIFE

That weekend, Mom got me a bus pass so I could get myself back and forth to Cathedral while she drove Georgia to her own school in a different part of the city.

But on Monday morning, she said she wanted to drive us both, just for the first day. I think she was more excited about Cathedral than I was.

"You've got your sketchbook?" she said.

"Right here," I said.

"And your good pen?"

"Got it."

"Should I come in with you?" she asked when we pulled up in front of the school.

"Nah, I'm good," I said. About a million kids were

hanging out on the sidewalk, and there was no way I was going to let them see my mommy walking me inside for the start of seventh grade.

"Okay, then. Well…" Mom kept looking at me the way she does when she's about to get all mushy. And then sure enough—

"You know, art school was always a dream of mine," she said. "And even though I never got to go, it feels like that dream is coming true right now. "

I was afraid she was going to start crying next. If there's one thing I can't deal with, it's when Mom cries, even the happy kind of tears.

But then—for once!—my sister's big mouth actually came in handy.

"Come on, come on, LET'S GO! We're going to be LATE!" Georgia screamed from the backseat, like there was some kind of lifesaving information handed out in the first ten minutes of fifth grade.

"All right," Mom said. "Well…good luck, honey!"

"Let's GOOOO!" Georgia said. "Rafe, get out!"

That was fine with me. Before Mom could kiss me good-bye in front of the whole school, I opened the car door and made my getaway. Then I headed straight inside for my first day as a real, live, actual art student.

Whatever that meant.

CHAPTER 16

FIRST DAY ON PLANET CATHEDRAL

When I walked inside the school, the first thing I saw was this huge painted banner that said WELCOME TO PLANET CATHEDRAL!

They weren't kidding either. The whole lobby was fixed up with little twinkly lights like stars, and a bunch of papier-mâché planets and asteroids hanging from the ceiling. There were kids playing weird, science-fictiony music on synthesizers, and all the teachers who were telling everyone where to go were wearing outfits made out of aluminum foil, like robot aliens. I guess it was some kind of first-day welcome-back-to-school thing.

That's when I knew for sure that I'd left Hills Village Middle School about eighty million light-years behind.

First up, I had something called New-Student Orientation. Basically, it was me and about a hundred sixth graders, learning everything there was to know about being a student at Cathedral School of the Arts.

After Mr. Crawley told us how happy we should be to be there (and I was!), they divided us up by program—theater, music, and visual arts. My group went with Mrs. Ling, the head of the art program, and she gave us a tour of that part of the school.

I guess if I had to pick one word to describe everything Mrs. Ling showed us on that tour, it would have to be...*totally, amazingly cooler than I ever expected.* (Lucky for me, I don't have to pick just one.) I couldn't wait to try everything I saw, and the more I saw, the more I wanted to try.

I mean, I was still going to have to get up and go to school five days a week. There was no way around that. Still—seventh grade was looking up, up, UP!

THE BiG CATCH
(AND I DON'T MEAN FiSH)

Except, of course, it wasn't exactly that simple. (It never is, right?)

After the tour, Mrs. Ling sat us all down in one of the art rooms and gave us a big talk.

It started off with the usual stuff about rules, and classes, and I'm not sure what else, because I wasn't exactly listening. I was still too excited about everything else.

But then, right near the end, she threw in the big catch.

"Boys and girls, I believe every one of you can do extremely well here," she said. *"However—*

"—not every student is invited back to Cathedral at the end of the year."

Now she had my attention. And there was more too.

"As some of you already know, all visual arts students at Cathedral are required to reapply for the program after our Spring Art Show in March," Mrs. Ling said. "In the meantime, if you can't keep up with your academic classes *and* your art assignments, *and* show us that you really want to be here, you might find yourself somewhere else next fall."

In other words, if I couldn't figure out a way to do this…

...then at the end of the year, I was going to be doing this:

To be honest, up until then I kind of thought it was a big deal that I had gotten into Cathedral at all. But it turned out that was the easy part.

Getting in was one thing.

Now I had to figure out how to *stay* in.

CHAPTER 18

THE STUFF OF ART

After orientation, my first three periods of the day were math, social studies, and…

You get the idea. All that stuff is just as boring in art school as it is anywhere else.

But then for fourth and fifth, every seventh grader had a double period of art, every single day. That meant ten periods a week I could actually look forward to, which was ten more than I had at Hills Village. Not too bad.

My first actual art class was drawing with Mr. Beekman, and let me tell you a few things about him. If there was ever a contest for world's oldest teacher, I'd definitely enter Mr. Beekman, and he might even win. He talked with an English accent and said stuff like "ladies and gentlemen" a lot.

The very first thing he ever said to us was this: ➡

Ladies and gentlemen, I am not here to teach you how to be artists.

So there it was, thirty seconds into my first art class, and I was already totally confused.

I was still trying to figure out that last part when Mr. Beekman turned on the slide projector and showed us a drawing of a big, fat horse. (At least, I think it was a horse. I wasn't sure about anything right then.)

"Twenty-three thousand years ago, someone created this image on the wall of a cave," Mr. Beekman said. "Now, who do you suppose was the artist here?"

"Was it you?" I heard someone say, too quietly for Beekman to hear.

"The answer, of course, is that we can't possibly know," he said.

"Even so, these early images *can* tell us quite a bit about the people who created them—the animals they hunted, the stories they told each other, the

62

elements of the world around them, and the objects of their everyday lives. Do you see?"

No, I did not.

Then Beekman turned around and wrote on the board: ART = LIFE = ART.

"In this class, I'll teach you about proper materials, line quality, composition—all the techniques you might use as artists. But the rest of it depends on what you bring to the table."

He was really getting into it now and walking all around the room. In fact, he didn't seem so old anymore either.

"What fascinates you? What life experiences have you had? What makes you *you*?" Beekman said. "Because *that*, ladies and gentlemen, is the true stuff of art!"

"I'm going to throw up the true stuff of breakfast in a second," the same kid from before said. This time, I looked over.

He was sitting all the way in the back, like me, drawing a fake tattoo on his arm while Beekman talked. And I'd say he was dressed weird, but this was Planet Cathedral. Weird is kind of its version of normal.

Meanwhile, Beekman was still going.

"With all of this in mind, your first assignment of the year will be a self-portrait," he said. Then he wrote on the board again: WHO ARE YOU?

"I want you to answer that question with your drawings. Then tomorrow in class, we'll have our first crit," he said. "Remember, ladies and gentlemen, bring your life to your art, and your art comes to life!"

I didn't understand half of the stuff he said, but all the other kids were nodding their heads like crazy. I mean, like, what the heck is a crit? And that's when I started to think maybe I'd missed out on more than just sixth grade at this place.

I was going to have to make up for some lost time.

CHAPTER 19

WHAT'S THE BiG IDEA?

That night, I stayed up late and did all my homework before I went to bed.

And no, you didn't just accidentally pick up someone else's book. This is still me, Rafe K. I just figured that the first day of the year was the wrong time to start falling behind.

But even then, after I finally turned out the light and tried to go to sleep, I couldn't stop thinking about everything.

I never thought art school would be so complicated. I just thought it would be, well, art and school. But now I had all this other stuff I had to think about. Like not getting kicked out, for instance. And getting a life in the meantime.

"Sounds like a mission to me," Leo said right away. "When do you want to start?"

This is the thing with Leo: There's no off switch. He's ready to go anytime.

Also, he loves a good mission.

The last one was called Operation R.A.F.E., which stood for Rules Aren't For Everyone, and it earned me an all-expenses-paid trip to summer school.

"Slow down," I said. "I can't start getting in trouble all over again. I promised Mom."

"No, you promised yourself," Leo reminded me. "Besides, who said anything about that? I'm talking about something better. Bigger!"

"Like what?"

"Like *real life*! All that 'stuff of art' Beekman was talking about. Maybe being an artist is supposed to be about more than just showing up at Cathedral every day and sleeping on this couch every night."

I couldn't argue with that part, but still—

"What am I supposed to do?" I said. "Just start... living?"

"You're closer than you think," Leo said. "It can be whatever you want. Ride the subway standing on your head. Eat chocolate-covered tarantulas. Go to twelve movies in a row. As long as you've never done it before, it's on the list."

"Hang on. There's a list?"

"We'll call it Operation: Get a Life. What do you think?"

That's another thing about Leo. He's always about a step and a half ahead of me.

"I think you're not the one who has to actually do all this stuff," I said. "Did you happen to notice all that homework? I can't start some whole new project now."

"Or," Leo said, "maybe you can't afford not to. Remember what Mrs. Ling said? 'Not every student is invited back.' I mean, unless you're trying to set some kind of record for getting kicked out of middle schools..."

I didn't know what to say to that. Instead, I just turned over and put a pillow on top of my head.

It wasn't like I thought Leo was wrong, exactly. It was more like, after the day I'd had, my brain felt like a stuffed mushroom, and there wasn't room for anything else.

"I'm going to sleep now," I said.

"I seriously doubt it," Leo said.

And, of course, he was right about that too.

CHAPTER 20

CRIT-iCAL CONDiTION

The next day, I found out what *crit* means.

It's short for *critique*, and it's an art school thing, where you have to put your assignment up in front of the whole class so everyone can talk about it. Kind of like getting up in front of a firing squad.

Actually, it's exactly like that.

Ready... Aim... CRIT!

I figured if I sat really still in the back and tried to blend in, Mr. Beekman might not call on me. But right near the end of fifth period, my luck ran out.

"Rafe...Khatchadorian," he said, looking at his attendance book. "Our new transfer student. Let's see what you have for us, shall we?"

He came over and took my self-portrait and stuck it on one of the bulletin boards at the front of the room.

"All right, everyone, let's have some comments. What does this portrait tell you about the artist?" Beekman said.

Right away, Zeke McDonald raised his hand. You haven't met him yet, so I'll just tell you right now—I hate Zeke McDonald. Him and all his friends. You know the type—the kids who walk around school like they've got invisible crowns on their heads? That's them. Zeke was basically good at everything, and he knew it, and he spent most of his time making sure everyone else knew it too.

Of course, I'd just gotten to Cathedral, so I didn't know enough to hate anyone yet. But that part was just about to start.

"Mr. Beekman," Zeke said, "I know Rafe wasn't

here last year, so should we take that into account with our crit? I mean, like the way his drawing is so…you know…basic?"

"You can critique the work on its own merits," Beekman said.

I wasn't sure what that meant, but obviously it had something to do with tearing me into little pieces, because right away Kenny Patel's hand popped up like a piece of toast. (He sits by Zeke in the front, which is all you need to know about him.)

"To be honest, I don't think Rafe's portrait tells us very much, except what he looks like," Kenny said. Then he turned around and looked back at me like there was a pile of doggy droppings on my chair. "Well, maybe not even that," he said, and a bunch of people laughed.

"Ladies and gentlemen, we *will* keep our critiques respectful," Beekman said, about five seconds too late. "If you have nothing constructive to add, then keep your comments to yourself. Now, how about some positive feedback? What do you see that you like about Rafe's drawing?"

And nobody...said...a *word*.

I think I heard a pin drop. Maybe some crickets. Also, the sound of my face turning the color of a stop sign. I could have farted out loud, and it would have been less embarrassing than the silence.

Finally, Beekman jumped in again.

"I think this is a good start, Mr. Khatchadorian," he said. "You've got a sure hand—I can see that. But I think you're holding back here. I'd like to see more of *Rafe* next time, do you understand?"

"Sure," I said, but honestly, I would have told him I was wearing ladies' underwear if it meant getting that crit over with faster.

And then, just when Beekman finally turned around to take my drawing off the board, good old Zeke McDonald held up his sketchbook for everyone else to see. He had drawn a portrait of *me*, and I sure didn't like it.

I've heard that every once in a while, there are these things called sinkholes that open up in the earth out of nowhere and swallow people whole. I don't know how often it happens, but right about then I was thinking, *Not nearly often enough*.

Maybe sometime before the next crit.

CHAPTER 21

BATHROOM BLUES

So if I told you I went straight to my locker, got my lunch, took it to the boys' bathroom, flushed my self-portrait down the toilet, and then ate my PB and J in one of the stalls, would you think I was a total loser?

Yeah, I thought so.

For me, bathrooms are kind of like bomb shelters. You can't live there forever, but they sure do come in handy sometimes.

"So what happens now?" Leo said.

"You're looking at it," I told him. Maybe it wasn't too late to transfer over to Meat Grinder Public Middle School.

"That's it? You're just going to give up?" he said. "You know what Jeanne Galletta would say, don't you?"

I knew, I knew. She'd say, "Don't give up—buck up." It's like her favorite expression. But that's easy for her to say. Jeanne's version of a bad day is an A-minus, or if the cafeteria runs out of chocolate milk.

Still, Jeanne is pretty smart.

For that matter, so is Leo. And I knew exactly what he was thinking right then. Operation: Get a Life was looking better and better, and more necessary, all the time.

"Okay, I'll think about it," I told him.

"Yes!"

"But that's all," I said. "I'm not making any—"

Just then the bathroom door opened, and someone came in.

I shut up quick and took my feet off the floor right away. I didn't want anyone to think I was sitting in here, pouting my way through lunch. Actually, I didn't want anyone to think I was sitting in here doing something else either.

One of the sinks came on next. I couldn't see who was there, but he left the water running for a really long time. In fact, I was just starting to think I was going to be stuck here all the time until sixth period, when it finally went off again.

I breathed about half a sigh of relief—until whoever it was walked right over and went into the stall beside mine.

A second later, I heard a voice. Not next to me. Above me.

"Hey."

I looked up, and it was the kid from drawing class. The one with the fake tattoo. He was standing there, I guess on the back of the other toilet, looking over the wall.

"What are you doing?" I said. "Get out of here!"

"They've got a name for that, you know," he said.

"Huh? A name for what?"

"At the crit. You just got *dinked*," the kid told me. "Don't take it personally. It's like a school sport around here. And Zeke McBonehead's the captain of the team."

*Dinked...crit...*it was like Planet Cathedral really did have its own secret language.

"Okay," I said. "Well, um...thanks." I didn't know what to say. He was just standing there, looking at me. "Anything else?"

"Yeah," the kid said. He held up something that

looked like a water balloon, except it wasn't, exactly. It was a rubber glove from one of the art rooms, filled up and tied off at the end. I thought for sure I was about to get it in the face.

But I didn't. Instead, the kid just smiled this evil kind of smile down at me.

Then he said, "You interested in a little revenge?"

CHAPTER 22

REVENGE IS SWEET (AND WET)

There were all kinds of reasons not to do this.
I couldn't afford to get in trouble. Mom would
kill me if she found out. I didn't even know if I
could trust this kid.

But I did like that word—*revenge*.

The kid didn't wait around for an answer either.
He went straight through the bathroom door and
kept going while I stood
there trying to figure
out what to do.

Then I decided it wasn't against the rules to follow someone out of a bathroom. So I kept going.

The kid was waiting for me across the hall, near a door to some stairs.

"Where are you going?" I asked. That whole school is like a big maze. I was still figuring it out.

"Up," he said.

When we got to the top, there were two more doors. One had a fire alarm on it, but the other opened right up. Inside was a big janitor's closet, with a window looking out onto the roof of the school. There was a metal grate over the window, with a lock, but the lock was already broken. And I was pretty sure I knew who had broken it.

The kid opened the grate, slid the window up, and climbed out onto the roof.

"Uh...I don't think we're supposed to go out there," I said.

"Uh...I don't think I see a sign," he said. "You coming?"

I'll tell you this much right now: If you could have turned around and gone back down those stairs, you're a better person than I am.

We stayed low all the way to the far side of the
roof, where we ducked behind the wall at the edge.
It was like we were part of a high-stakes war...or
at least an intense game of paintball.

The kid held up two fingers and pointed over the
wall for me to take a look. Sure enough, Zeke and
Kenny were right there, sitting at the top of the
bleachers like they were on their own personal throne.

My heart was beating out a major drum solo by
now, but I gave the kid a thumbs-up anyway.

He opened his backpack and handed me two of

those rubber-glove balloons. Then he took out two more for himself. I saw that he'd drawn bloodshot eyes right onto them, with red and black permanent markers. He'd even signed his own work with what I guessed were his initials—MTF.

What I didn't know yet was that this kid had the world's most perfect nickname. Everyone at Cathedral called him Matty the Freak. Nice to meet you, Mr. Freak.

Next, he took out a little piece of wire and poked a tiny hole in each glove. "So they'll break and not just bounce," he said.

That was basically the point of no return, like lighting a fuse. The next thing I knew, Matty the Freak was tossing his two water bombs over the edge.

And the *next* thing I knew, so was I.

I didn't get to see what happened, but I heard it anyway—four big splashes and a whole lot of yelling. We were already tearing back across the roof, through that janitor's closet window, and onto the stairs so we could laugh our butts off in private.

"That was amazing," I said.

"Hey," the kid told me, "it's the stuff of art, right?"

He didn't even know how right he was.

Operation: Get a Life had just officially begun.

CHAPTER 23

OPERATION: GET a LIFE

I stayed up late again that night, but not for homework.

Now that Operation: Get a Life was actually going to happen, Leo and I needed to figure out what the whole thing should look like.

The basic idea was super simple. We decided that every time I did something I'd never done before, it was going to count as part of the mission. That was it. No points this time, no bonuses, no lives to lose. If I got back into Cathedral at the end of the year—mission accomplished. And if not—welcome to Loserville.

The next thing I did was look at a calendar. There were 195 days to go until the Spring Art

Show at school, on March 23. After that I'd have to reapply, and I was either in or out. So I decided I was going to have to do 195 things I'd never done before—at least one new thing every single day.

One hundred and ninety-five chances to Get a Life.

"And I'm bringing back the No-Hurt Rule too," I told Leo. "Same as last year. No one gets hurt from any of this stuff I'm going to do. If that happens, it's game over."

"Yeah, okay, but you still get credit for today," Leo said. "That rule wasn't in place when you dropped those balloons on Zeke's and Kenny's heads."

I decided I could live with that. But I did have a few other conditions.

"I'm including myself in the No-Hurt Rule this time," I said. "If I get a detention, it's one week of time out. If I get suspended—game over. And most of all, if Mom finds out about any of this—"

"Yeah, yeah, I get it. Game over," Leo said. "I think I'm bored already."

But I wasn't budging on that one. The last thing Mom needed right now was to start worrying about me all over again. And the last thing *I* needed was for her to think I was up to my old tricks.

Even if I wasn't. Technically, this mission was like the opposite of the last one. The whole idea back then was to break as many school rules as possible. This time around, it was about keeping me *in* school, but something told me Mom might not see it like that. After the way things went in sixth grade, I was pretty sure she'd put me up for adoption if she even heard the words *mission* and *Rafe* anywhere near each other.

"So we'll just have to make sure she never finds out," Leo said. "And that means Georgia too, because her mouth is about as big as the city."

Again, I could live with that. No Hurt, no Mom, no Georgia— no problem.

And in the meantime, game on!

CHAPTER 24

GREAT, BAD, WORSE

The second day of Operation: Get a Life started out great. Right before it turned bad. And then got even worse.

But first, the good part: Mom let me take the bus to school by myself for the first time. And I'm not talking about the big piece of yellow cheese I rode in sixth grade. I'm talking about an actual city bus.

It felt really weird (in a good way) to ride through the city alone like that.

I kept looking around at all the zillions of other people and thinking about how I was one of them now.

Rafe Khatchadorian, city kid. Who'd have thunk it?

So by the time I got to school, I'd already done my at-least-one-new-thing for the day, and I was just getting started. As far as I could tell, I was going to knock this whole mission right out of the park.

And then I got to my locker. (Here comes the bad part.)

It all looked normal enough from the outside, but once I turned the combination and opened the door, it looked like some kind of alien creature had crawled in there during the night, swallowed a hand grenade, and exploded all over everything.

Okay, it was just green paint, but still—my social studies book was green,

my notebooks were green, my gym stuff was green; and all of it was dripping, wet, sticky, and gross. Someone had figured out a way to pump about a gallon in through the vents on the door.

And by *someone*, I mean Zeke McDonald and Kenny Patel, the left and right butt cheeks of Cathedral School of the Arts. When I looked around, they were right there, hanging out by the stairs. Zeke had his phone pointed at me, and both of them cracked up as soon as I saw them. Then they just turned and walked away.

And I thought, *Revenge is a two-way street, isn't it?* Maybe those water balloons were a bad idea after all.

It wasn't over either. I was still standing there trying to figure out how I was going to unpaint the inside of my locker, when the PA system came on in the hall, and the bad part of my morning got shoved aside for the even worse part.

May I have your attention, please? Rafe Khatchadorian, please report to Mr. Crawley's office immediately. Thank you, and have a terrible day.

THE CRAWLEY

Five minutes later, I stumble into The Crawley's lair, far beneath the surface of Planet Cathedral.

It's dark down here. Too dark to really see where I'm going. I hear dripping water somewhere, and there's a bad smell in the air, like a sandwich made out of old cheese…and death.

My feet feel their way across the rocks as I go. "Hello?" I say. "Anybody here?"

"Good morning," a voice answers from the shadows. "Come in, please."

I take another step—but it's one too many. The ground slips away beneath me, and the next thing I know, I'm falling through empty air.

The place where I land is soft but sticky. Long

strands like superglue-covered ropes grab on to my arms and legs and don't let go. I struggle, but that only makes things worse. Before I've even started to put up a fight, I'm completely immobilized in The Crawley's web.

He's not even trying to appear human down here. Why should he? I'm on his turf now—and at his mercy. One quick stab with those razor-sharp pincers, and he could drain me like a juice box.

"And how are you this morning, Rafe?" he asks, cool as an eight-legged cucumber.

"I'm okay," I tell him. It's important that I stay calm too. They say The Crawley can smell fear a mile away.

They also say he likes to play with his food before he eats it.

"I want to ask you about a little incident we had yesterday," he says. "Something involving a couple of water balloons?"

Not water balloons, I think. *Rubber gloves.* Of course, I'm not stupid. The less I say here, the better.

"Do you know anything about that?" he asks me.

"I heard about it," I say.

"That's all?" he says. "So you don't know who was responsible?"

"No, sir."

I may be totally unarmed, but there is one weapon I can use. It's called *denial*. As long as The

Crawley doesn't have any proof, I still have a small chance of getting out of here alive.

He starts to circle the lair. I can't even turn my mummified head, so I lose sight of him for a minute.

When he comes around again, there's something in his hand.

"Do you know what this is, Rafe?" he says. At first, it looks like a plain folder. Then I see my name, and the words HILLS VILLAGE MIDDLE SCHOOL across the front. "It seems you had quite a year last year. Got into a bit of trouble on your home planet, did you?"

My mind scrambles for something to say.

"That was all just a misunderstanding," I tell him. "I've changed since then. I turned over a new leaf. That's not me anymore...."

Now I'm saying too much. I can tell he's not buying it. I try to look him in the eye, but it's hard to know which of those six eyes to look into.

"Rafe, I'm going to ask you one more time," he says. "Are you sure you don't know anything about all this?"

"I'm sure!" I tell him. "I swear!"

The lair goes quiet as he stares me down for a

good long time. All I can hear now are those pincers clicking away, ready to start slicing and dicing at any moment.

But then The Crawley reaches up and cuts right through the threads of his own web. A second later, I fall out onto the floor in a heap.

"You can go," he says.

Already I'm back on my feet, running for daylight as fast as I can.

"But I've got my eye on you, Rafe!" he screeches after me. "I'd hate to see what happens if you land in here again!"

Yeah, I think. Him and me both.

CHAPTER 26

COVERT OPS

By the time I left Mr. Crawley's office, everything had changed. I wasn't just the new transfer student at Cathedral anymore. Now I was the new troublemaker, as far as he was concerned.

I don't understand how this keeps happening to me. I've never been very good at being good, if you know what I mean, but sometimes it's like all the trouble in the world is made of metal, and I'm just one big walking magnet. I could change schools every two weeks, and it wouldn't matter. That permanent record of mine might as well be tattooed across my forehead.

And then, just when I thought my morning couldn't get any weirder, it did.

I was headed straight up the hall to first period when someone grabbed me from behind. The next thing I knew, I was pulled into some kind of broom closet, the door slammed shut, and everything went pitch-black.

I didn't wait around for instructions. I just started swinging. I figured if this was Zeke and Kenny, I might as well do as much damage as I could before they got me.

But then I heard "Ow! OW! Cut it out! It's me—Matty!"

"Huh?" I stopped with my fist in the air. "What are you doing?" I asked him.

"I wanted to know why you got called to the office," he said, like it was completely normal to have a conversation in a pitch-dark closet. (And for all I know, it *was* normal—for Matty.)

"Why do you think?" I said. "Crawley basically knows I dropped those balloons off the roof."

"Rubber gloves," Matty said.

"Whatever."

"And what'd you tell him?" he asked.

"Nothing," I said. "He couldn't prove it, so I just kept my mouth shut."

I don't know if this will make sense, but I swear I heard Matty smile right there in the dark.

"Awesome," he said.

"Yeah, for you. Meanwhile, Zeke and Kenny trashed my locker."

Now I heard him laughing. "Don't worry about them. There's still plenty of time for that little war."

"I don't want a little war," I said. "I don't want any kind of war. I just want to get to first period. Crawley's going to be watching me like I'm free HBO from now on."

"Yeah, all right." Matty cracked the door open and checked the hall for me. "But I owe you one. If you ever change your mind, I've got your back."

It wasn't until I was walking away that I even realized something good might have come out of this after all.

Unless I was mistaken, I'd just made a real, live human friend for the first time since I started middle school. (And no, Jeanne Galletta doesn't count. She was my math tutor, for one thing, and she might have been *friendly*, but we were never *friends*. At least, not for her.)

Matty said it himself—*I've got your back.*

That has to be worth something, doesn't it?

TIPS FOR SURVIVAL

Flash forward!

If I tried to write down everything that happened during that first quarter at Cathedral, you'd need a wheelbarrow to carry this book around. So I'm going to skip over some stuff.

The short version is this: I spent a lot of time just getting used to my new school, new home, new city—and I learned a ton, usually the hard way. Here are some handy FYIs, just in case you ever find yourself in the same situation.

NUMBER ONE

When you're the only boy in a small house with one grandmother, one mother, one sister, and one bathroom, all I can say is—learn how to be patient. Oh, and plan ahead.

NUMBER TWO

Art isn't easy! It turns out there are just as
many rules for making art in art school as there
are for anything else. If you don't believe me, just
try holding your paintbrush the wrong way in
Mrs. Grundewald's class sometime, and see what
happens.

NUMBER THREE

Art school is smart school. As far as I can tell, most of the kids at Cathedral were born with a math book in one hand and an extra brain in the other. So if you're a dummy like me, don't expect to blend in! (And just in case you're wondering, the answer is *yes*, all those famous dead artists had to learn pre-algebra too. At least, that's what Mr. Frum told me when I asked.)

NUMBER FOUR

You want to live in the big city? Man up! People here will walk right over you if you let them...

...so don't let them.

NUMBER FIVE

What are you listening to me for? If you've been paying attention, then you'll know that your best bet is to very carefully watch everything I do—and then do exactly the opposite. Because my paths tend to lead to trouble.

(Just don't say I never warned you.)

Okay, got it? Good.

Oh, and *you're welcome.*

MY NEW LIFE, STEP 1

It turns out when you've got a new home, new city, and new school, it's not exactly hard to find new experiences. I was scooping them up without even trying —which was all great for my mission. In the meantime, here are some of the highlights, lowlights, and everything-in-between-lights of Operation: Get a Life.

CHAPTER 29

LEO TURNS UP THE HEAT

I'm not saying that five Cs and a B-minus make me some kind of genius, but those were the best grades I'd ever gotten. With Mom home all the time, she was around to help me with my homework and to make sure I did all my assignments, whether I wanted to or not.

And Operation: Get a Life was going even better. By the time report cards came out, I had 58 things on my list, with 137 to go. I figured I must be doing something right.

But Leo figured otherwise.

"You've got to step this mission up," he told me. "It's time to start thinking bigger."

"What are you talking about?" I said. "I've got this whole huge list already."

"It's called Operation: Get a Life, not Operation: Get a List. Most of that stuff is just about classes you have to go to anyway, and walking around the city on a leash with Mom. You're not even trying to make this interesting."

"Oh, man. Here we go," I said.

This is what Leo does. He calls it making things *interesting*, but I call it a pain the butt.

"New rule," he said. "From now on, you have to do at least one really big thing for every ten little things. And no more credit for the little stuff until you do."

"Hang on—what counts as a big thing?" I said.

Of course he had an answer. He always does. "For starters, it has to be something you'll remember doing for the rest of your life," he said.

"Oh, that's all?"

"No, actually. It also can't be anything you do at school, and there can't be some adult looking over your shoulder while you're doing it."

On top of all that, I still had the No-Hurt Rule to worry about, and none of this stuff could cost money either, because I didn't have any.

Still, Leo had a point. If this mission was going

to be worth doing, I needed to do it right. It was time to step up my game. I just didn't have any clue what that was going to look like yet.

And then a few days later, Mrs. Ling gave us the junk-sculpture assignment.

CHAPTER 30

ANOTHER WAY OF LOOKING AT IT

Take a look at this," Mrs. Ling said, and showed us a picture of an old garbage can.

"And now this," she said.

"And this," she said. "And this.

"Quite often, the artist's job is to show the world something familiar, but in a whole new way," she said. "That's your assignment this week. I want you all to take at least one object that might look like junk to anyone else, and give it a new life, as art."

I guess I'd been going to Cathedral long enough now, because I actually understood what Mrs. Ling was talking about. I liked the idea of giving something a whole new life. Kind of what I was trying to do with me these days.

As usual, I was sitting in the back with Matty. He was already sketching ideas like crazy, but then he scribbled something on the corner of his page, tore it off, and passed it over to me.

After class, he told me there were a bunch of places he knew where people threw away good junk all the time.

"And we can just take it?" I said. "Are you sure?"

"Relax. We're looking for garbage, not robbing a bank," he said. "You worry too much, you know that?"

I thought that was kind of funny, since most people think I don't worry enough.

Still, he let me use his phone to call Mom. I told her I was going to be working on an art assignment after school, and she was all over it. She just asked if I wanted her to come pick me up later.

"I'll take the bus," I said.

Technically, there weren't any lies in there. I just left out the part about where I was going to be, partly because I didn't think Mom would like it, and partly because I didn't know.

I wasn't even sure what Dumpster diving was, exactly, but it sounded like fun. It also sounded like just the kind of thing Leo thought I needed more of for my list.

And it was.

CHAPTER 31

WELCOME TO DUMPSTER DIVING

CHAPTER 32

THE BIG PICTURE

When I got home that night, the first thing I thought was—

HOLY CROW, WE'VE BEEN ROBBED!

The closet in the front hall was hanging open, there was stuff all over the floor, and Grandma's place looked like a wreck.

Well...*even more* of a wreck than usual.

"Rafe? Is that you?" Mom yelled. "We're back here!"

I followed the trail of stuff like Hansel and Gretel on those bread crumbs and found everyone in the kitchen. Mom was shoving piles of newspaper into a garbage bag, Georgia was clomping around in a big pair of high-heeled shoes, and Grandma was at the table, looking through a bunch of old pictures in a shoe box.

"What's going on?" I said.

"Spring cleaning!" Grandma said, even though it was only November. "It's time we emptied some of these closets and made a little room for you three around here."

I guess that was supposed to be good news. I'd been using my suitcase as a dresser, and most of our stuff was still in that storage locker in Hills Village.

But actually, it wasn't good news at all. Ever since we moved to the city, Mom had been talking about finding a job first, and then a bigger place for all four of us to live. But so far—no job. And now it seemed that we weren't going anywhere soon. I could tell Mom was thinking the same thing, just by looking at her.

"Hey, kiddos, have I ever shown you my old photos?" Grandma said. "Come over here and take a walk down memory lane. See what a cute baby your mom was?"

Georgia went over to see, but I was still watching Mom. The way she kept stuffing more paper into that bag, I thought it was going to break right open.

"Here's another good one," Grandma said. "Jules,

take a look. It's you and Ralph in front of Hairy's Place."

That got my attention. I thought Grandma meant me when she said "Ralph"—but then I saw the picture.

"Who is that?" Georgia said.

"It's Dad," I told her. I guess she wouldn't even remember what he looked like. "Except I thought his name was Luca."

"It is," Mom said. She was still cleaning and never looked at the picture even once. "Ralph's his middle name."

"Oh," I said. "I didn't know that."

But it did explain a few things—like why Grandma kept calling me that. So maybe she was only sort of crazy and not completely mashed potatoes.

In the picture, my father had his arm around Mom, and it looked like they were still in high school. I'd never seen this one before. Actually, I'd never seen many pictures of my father, period. I think Mom threw them all away when he left.

We hardly ever talked about him anymore. It was kind of a touchy subject, and whenever I used

to ask, Mom always said the same thing: "That's a short story." After a while I got the hint and stopped asking.

Basically, the story went like this: My father left when I was four and Georgia was two. That was about a year after Leo died. Once he was gone, we never heard from him again. End of story.

Until now, anyway.

"Did you know Hairy is still in business?" Grandma said to Mom. "All the way over there on Calumet Avenue."

At first, Mom looked like she was going to say

something. But then she set down the garbage bag, took a deep breath, and walked out of the kitchen. A few seconds later, I heard the bathroom door close upstairs.

"What just happened?" Georgia asked. "Is she mad about something?"

Grandma pulled Georgia up onto her lap. "I think your mom's having a bad day," she said. "That's all."

But that wasn't all. Not for me, anyway. I was pretty sure I'd just figured out what my next big thing was going to be.

And Hairy's seemed like a pretty good place to start.

CHAPTER 33

QUESTIONS, QUESTIONS

Maybe this sounds weird, but I didn't really spend much time thinking about my father before all this. Most of my life, he didn't really exist. I mean, not for us, anyway. I was used to not having him around.

But now, after seeing that picture, I couldn't *stop* thinking about him. What did he look like? Did he live in the city? Was he rich? Poor? Did he think about us much?

Mission complete. Send the jet!

TOP SECRET

I sat up late that night, drawing in my sketchbook and talking to Leo about it.

"What do you think will happen if I find him?" I said.

"I don't know, but I'll give you a ton of credit for the mission," he said.

Sometimes Leo has a one-track mind.

"What happens if I look for him and *don't* find him?" I said.

"What if you stop asking questions and start figuring it out?" Leo said.

So as soon as I heard Grandma's TV go off upstairs, I got out of bed and went over to the computer.

spare change?

I couldn't find a website for Hairy's Place, but I did find an address—3921 Calumet Avenue. I pulled it up on a map and then coughed a lot while it was printing out, just in case Mom was still awake.

Then I stuck the map in the bottom of my backpack and tried to get some sleep.

Even that wasn't easy, though. On top of everything else, I started thinking about that question Mr. Beekman put up on the board the first day of school: *WHO ARE YOU?* Like maybe if I could find out more about who my father was, I might find out more about me too.

And if that wasn't part of getting a life, I didn't know what was.

SCARY HAiRY

The next day, when I asked Matty how to get to the corner of Calumet Avenue and Thirty-Third Street, he got right on board. First thing after school, we were back out on the streets. He showed me how to get the number 23 bus and then the number 9 bus to get to the place I'd marked on the map.

I didn't tell him why I was doing this, but it didn't even seem like it mattered. Matty the Freak was always up for anything.

As soon as we got off the bus, Hairy's Place was right there on the corner. It looked pretty much like the picture Grandma showed me, but I didn't know it was a barbershop until I saw it in person.

"I get it," Matty said. "*Hairy's* Place."

"Wait out here. I'll be right back," I told him.

Now he got curious. "Why? What are you doing, anyway?"

"I'm robbing a bank," I said. "Just wait outside, okay?"

It was either that or tell him I was looking for someone who got his picture taken on this corner about twenty years ago. Yeah, that doesn't sound too ridiculous.

Inside the shop, there were three barber chairs lined up in front of a big mirror, but only one barber. I knew the second I saw him it had to be Hairy, since he was so…well, *hairy*. And huge too. He looked like Bigfoot with tattoos.

"Pop a squat, kid," he said. "I'll be right with you."

"Oh. Uh…okay," I said.

I sat down in one of the regular chairs near the front and picked up a *Field & Stream* magazine. Even that seemed kind of weird to me. I hadn't seen a single field, or a stream, since I'd moved to the city.

But before I could even crack it open, Matty came strolling in from the street.

"We got a line going," Hairy told him. "You can wait if you want."

"Sounds good," Matty said. Then he sat down a few chairs away from me like we didn't even know each other. I was giving him the evil eye the whole time, but he was evil eye–proof. He just sat there holding a magazine upside down and watching to see what I'd do.

Whatever, I thought. I wasn't going to turn back now. The other customer was already paying for his haircut, and Hairy was waving me over with this big pair of scissors in his hand.

"Next!" he said.

"Actually," I said, "I just wanted to ask you about something."

Right away Hairy's face went all mean, and those two bushy eyebrows of his turned into one big shrub.

"This ain't a library," he said. "You want to pay for a cut, we can talk all you want. Otherwise, I got customers waiting."

I was pretty sure a haircut would cost more than thirty-five cents, which is what I had in my pocket. Meanwhile, my throat was starting to feel like a clogged drain.

"Oh...um...I mean...I just wanted to ask if you knew—"

"Did I stutter?" he said. Or more like roared. "Stop wasting my time, Shrimpo! I've got bills to pay!"

I didn't know what to say to that, but Matty sure did.

"Hey, mister," he said. "I'm just curious. What's it like to be the world's tallest butt-wipe?"

That was pretty much the end of the conversation. Hairy came right for us then, looking like he was ready to kill. (And did I already mention those scissors?)

One thing I'll say for myself—I'm pretty fast on my feet. I hit that sidewalk in about half a second flat and didn't stop running for the next six miles. Or maybe it was three blocks, I don't know.

Matty was still laughing when he caught up to me.

"Did you see the look on that guy's face?" he said. "Grumpiest barber ever, no contest."

I guess I could have been mad about him messing things up, but I was actually glad Matty was there. Besides, it wasn't like Bigfoot Hairy was about to sit me down and break out the milk and cookies.

"But I don't get why he acted like that," Matty said. "I thought he was related to you or something."

"Related to me?" I said. I figured Matty had to be joking, but he looked totally serious. "What are you talking about?"

"His name was right there on the mirror, next to his picture. Didn't you see that?"

"What name?" I said.

"Harold Khatchadorian," Matty said. "Why didn't you ever tell me you were part giant before?"

SPILLING
(SOME OF) THE BEANS

So that's when I told Matty everything.

Well, not *everything*. I didn't mention Leo. There aren't too many people I trust in the world, besides Mom (and Leo, of course), but even if there were, I wouldn't exactly start off by telling them about my imaginary best friend.

Still, I did tell him about my dad, and why we went to Hairy's, and even about Operation: Get a Life.

I thought Matty might laugh or something when I was done talking, but he didn't even flinch.

"And you're doing all that just so you can stay at Cathedral School of the Farts for another year?" he said. "How come?"

"Don't you like it there?" I said.

"Compared to what? I mean, it's better than regular school. But, dude—it's still school."

I thought that was a pretty good answer. In fact, the more I got to know this kid, the more I liked him.

"You know what?" Matty said. "Forget about Hairy. Forget about all that stuff. You want to live a little? Come on."

He was already walking back toward the bus stop. And then he was running again. Now it was my turn to try to keep up.

"Where are we going?" I said.

Matty didn't even look back. He just kept running.

"Everywhere!" he said.

CHAPTER 36

BEST. DAY. EVER!

I learned a few things about Matty the Freak that day. Things like:

His real name was Matthew Theodore Fleckman.

He came up with his own nickname, Matty the Freak, so that MTF worked either way.

He had three younger brothers, a mom, a dad, and a beagle. The beagle's name was Bagel.

And most important of all, I learned that Matty Fleckman knew how to do more stuff for no money than anyone I'd ever met.

When we got off the bus again, our first stop was the biggest Electronics Depot Warehouse you've ever seen. This place practically had its own ZIP code. The whole third floor was just games, and almost all of them were set up so you could try them right there in the store.

"You just have to keep moving," Matty told me. "Then they don't know how long you've been here, and you can play all day if you want."

After that, we hit the megaplex just up the street. It was the kind of place with superluxury seating, where you could spend a hundred dollars on snacks without even getting full, and the tickets cost fifteen bucks each.

Unless, of course, you're Matty the Freak.

We walked right past the main entrance and around to the side of the building, where there were a bunch of one-way exit doors with no handles on the outside. No problem, though. The theater had something like thirty-eight screens, so it didn't take long before a movie let out and a bunch of people started coming out the doors.

"Just be cool and follow my lead," Matty said. Then he walked right into the crowd, like we were swimming upstream.

"Mom?" he started saying. "*Mom?* Excuse me, have you seen a tall lady with a red hat?"

I thought Leo the Silent was a genius, but this was the best move I'd ever seen. Two minutes later, we were up to our eyeballs in superluxury seating at the first R-rated movie I'd ever watched in a theater. It was called *Zombomania* and, believe me, I saw some stuff I definitely wasn't supposed to—for instance, a lady who not only was a zombie but also happened to have no clothes on—the whole time.

And all I can say to that is—!!!!!!!!!!!!!!

So all of that was pretty good already. But then, when the movie let out, we were starving, and Matty said he knew a place where we could get something to eat—for free, of course.

"Sounds good to me," I said. "Where to?"

DOTTY ON THE LINE

So how's that junk sculpture coming along?" Mom asked me while I was pretending to be hungry for dinner that night. "You've been working so hard on it lately."

I told her the sculpture was going okay, which was true, but meanwhile I was also trying to erase the last five hours from my brain. I don't know about you, but my mother's like a mind reader that way. It's safer if you just don't think about the stuff you don't want her to know.

And that wasn't easy, because I still had about a hundred questions I wanted to ask.

Finally, after dinner, I decided to take a chance—
not with Mom but with Grandma. I waited until
Mom and Georgia were upstairs watching a movie,
and then I found Grandma in the living room,

fixing up the couch for me the way she did every night.

"Grandma?" I said. I kept my voice down, just in case.

"Yeah, kiddo?"

"You know that picture of Mom with my dad? The one of them in front of Hairy's Place?"

"Sure. I love that picture," she said.

"Well, I was just curious. Do you know who Hairy is? I mean, not that it really matters or anything," I said.

"Oh, he's your father's uncle," she said, just like that. "Not a very nice man, though." Then she went back to tucking my blankets in under the cushions.

It hit me like a punch in the stomach. That big, hairy—scary—guy was *my great-uncle*? It seemed kind of impossible, even though it wasn't impossible at all.

"Grandma?" I said again.

"Yeah, kiddo?"

"Do you know what his real name is?"

"Whose name, sweetie?" she said. Sometimes talking to Grandma is a little like a bad phone connection.

"Hairy," I said. "The guy with the barbershop. The one in the old picture?"

Grandma got this big smile on her face. "You know, that reminds me," she said. "Have I ever shown you my old photos before? We should dig them out sometime and take a little walk down memory lane."

Well, what was I going to say to that? Besides, it wasn't like going back to square one. I already knew more than I did before I talked to her.

"Sure," I told her. "That sounds good."

She dropped a couple of pillows onto the couch and then crunched me up in one of those surprisingly strong hugs of hers.

"I love you, Ralphie," she said. "You're a good boy."

"I love you too, Grandma," I said.

And that was the truth too.

HERE WE GO AGAIN

I decided to leave the whole Hairy thing alone for a while and give him some time to cool off. Like maybe until the next ice age.

But I wasn't quitting either. That night after Grandma went upstairs, I got right back on the computer.

This time, I typed in *Luca Khatchadorian* to see what I could find.

There wasn't much, though. Almost all of it was about some kid who lived on a goat farm in some place called Latvia.

So I tried just plain *Khatchadorian* after that, but then it was the opposite problem: I got about two million hits.

Finally, I searched for *Ralph Khatchadorian*, just

for the heck of it. That got me a big zero, but the message on the screen also said *Did you mean "Rafe Khatchadorian?"*

And I thought—I don't know…did I?

I figured it couldn't hurt to click anyway.

The first thing on the list that came up had my name right there, and something about Cathedral. Then, when I clicked on that, it brought up my student page on the school's site, with a bunch of pictures, artwork, and other stuff.

The only problem was, I didn't *have* a student page on the school's site. I knew we were allowed to set them up, but the only people who did that were the ones who had eighteen thousand friends they could collect and show off.

And whoever had set up this page was no friend of mine.

Rafe Khatchadorian

About Me

HOMETOWN Somewhere under a rock

FAVORITE ACTIVITIES Picking my nose (also my favorite lunch!); Wishing I was someone else; Wondering what it's like to talk to girls; Hiding in the bathroom during lunch

FAVORITE ARTIST me, me, ME!!!!!!!!!!!!!!!!!!!!!!!!!

FAVORITE QUOTE I need my diaper changed...

My Pics

You've had 9 1 0 Visitors

click for video

R a f e K. = faKeR

Rafe K. fReaK

145

The more I looked at it, the more I forgot why I had sat down at the computer in the first place. I wasn't thinking about Luca Ralph Khatchadorian anymore. Now I was thinking about Zeke McDonald and Kenny Patel.

And revenge.

Again.

"Hey, Leo?" I said.

"What's up?" he said.

"I need to call a time-out in Operation: Get a Life."

"WHAT?"

"Just for a few days," I told him.

"Why?"

"Because of the No-Hurt Rule," I said. "I think I'm about to break it, and I don't want to be in the game when I do."

CHAPTER 39

W-A-R

CHAPTER 40

Re-Revenge

The next day at lunch, I took Matty into the computer lab and showed him the fake page Zeke and Kenny had made.

Before you could say "payback," he already had an idea. He pulled out his notebook right there and started drawing, really fast, the way he always does.

"We're going to get them back the same way they got you," he said.

"You mean like another web page?" I said.

"No, something better," he said. "But when it happens, they're going to know exactly who did it to them, and they'll never be able to prove it."

See, this is why it's good to have a professional

freak on your side. I didn't even know what Matty's idea was, and I already liked it.

Meanwhile, he just kept scribbling and drawing, scribbling and drawing.

"So, the junk-sculpture crit is this Friday, right?" he said. "That means Thursday fifth period, everyone's going to be finishing their sculptures and leaving them in the back of Mrs. Ling's room."

"Yeah?" I said. "And?"

"What time does fifth period let out?"

"Eleven forty-five," I told him, because I always know when lunch is.

Matty wrote *Ling* and *11:45* on two different parts of the page. That's when I realized what he was drawing. It was a map of the school. But I still didn't understand why.

"I'm thinking we'll need maybe five minutes before Mrs. Ling comes down," he said, and wrote that too. "Then maybe another three minutes until—"

"Slow down a second," I said. "You've got to catch me up here. What happens at eleven forty-five on Thursday?"

Finally, Matty put down his pen and gave me this look like he was sitting on the world's best secret. Which he kind of was.

"Just the first professional art-napping in the history of Cathedral School of the Arts," he said. "That's all."

CHAPTER 41

A REALLY GOOD PLAN

If you haven't already noticed, Matty the Freak never does anything halfway. That's one of the things I liked about him. By fifth period that Thursday, we had the whole plan figured out, right down to the last detail.

OPERATION:

ART~ NAP!

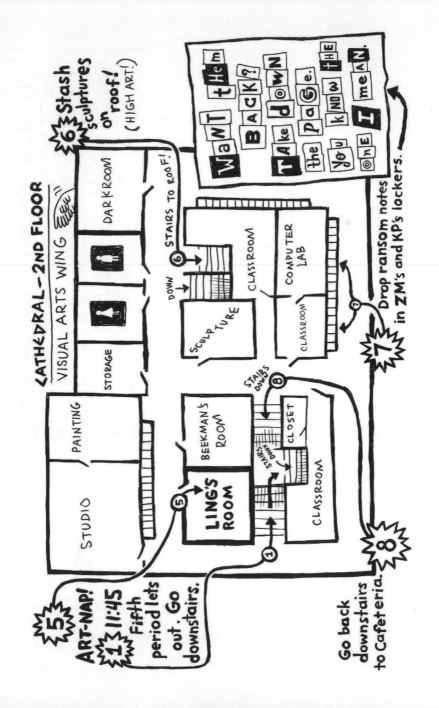

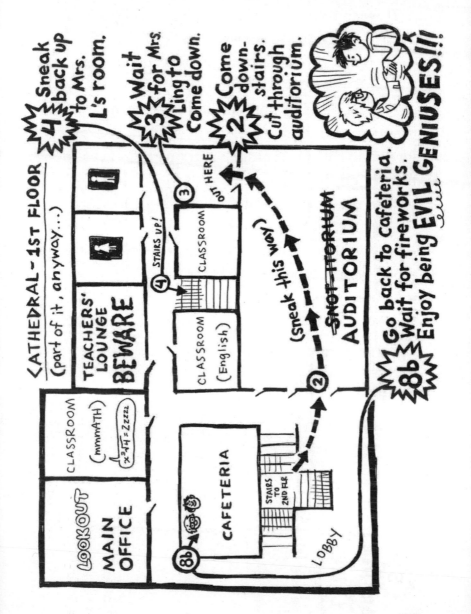

153

It wasn't like we were going to *keep* Zeke's and Kenny's sculptures. We were just going to hide them up on the roof until they took down that stupid RAFE K page of theirs. As soon as they did, they'd get another note in their lockers, telling them where to look. If they knew what was good for them, the whole thing would be taken care of by the crit on Friday.

And Matty was right. It didn't matter whether they knew this was coming from me or not. In fact, I wanted them to. This was war, after all—the kind where you're supposed to know exactly who your enemy is.

I know I sure did.

CHAPTER 42

OPERATION: ART-NAP

All through fifth period that day, I could barely concentrate on finishing my own sculpture. I'd made a little couch out of pieces of scrap wood. Then I'd made a little man out of wire and covered him with a thin piece of aluminum that I molded like a blanket. It wasn't a self-portrait, exactly, but I was trying to "bring my life to my art," like Mr. Beekman was always telling us to do. I called it *Kid Sleeping on Couch*. (I couldn't think of anything else.)

Finally, the bell rang for lunch. Operation: Art-nap was a go!

First, Matty and I put our sculptures on the back table and headed downstairs, like everyone else. But then, when no one was looking, we cut around through the auditorium and out the other side. That's where we could watch for Mrs. Ling in the hallway. As soon as she came around the corner with her lunch tray and went into the teachers' lounge, we headed upstairs again. Thirty seconds later, we were back in Mrs. L.'s room, and it was totally deserted.

So far, so good. Matty grabbed Kenny's sculpture, and I took Zeke's.

Kenny had made a palm tree out of a plastic pipe and a broken umbrella, all covered with cut-up pieces of cereal boxes that he painted brown and green. It looked okay, I guess.

And as for Zeke's sculpture—well, you'd have to torture me and *then* pay me a thousand bucks to say I liked anything about Zeke McDonald. But he was obviously going to get an A, like always.

First, he'd built this metal cube out of steel rods and hot glue. Then he strung the whole thing with fishing line and hung about a million little rusted screws and gears and springs inside. It was like a mobile in a cage, and it made this cool sound if you blew on it.

And yeah, okay, it was maybe just a little...tiny... bit...awesome.

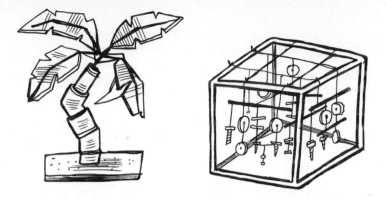

Still, all I could think about was how Zeke's and Kenny's brains were going to melt right out their ears when they found out their art had been 'napped. I threw my sweatshirt over the cube to keep it from making too much noise, and we headed straight for the door.

That's when we hit our first roadblock.

As soon as I checked the hall, I saw one of the janitors, Mr. McQuade. He was parking his big rolling trash can outside the boys' bathroom—which was also right across from the stairs to the roof, where we needed to go.

I stepped back and pointed. "What do we do?" I whispered.

Just then, Mr. McQuade opened the bathroom door and went inside.

"Go!" Matty said. *"Now!"*

Before I could think about it, he went out ahead of me, and I followed him up the hall. All we needed was half a minute to get past that door and up to the roof.

And then—roadblock number two.

When Matty got to the stairs, he stopped short. I almost crashed into him, and Zeke's sculpture started clanging under my sweatshirt. My heart started clanging pretty hard too.

WHAT? I said, not even talking, just mouthing it now.

Matty pointed down, and mouthed back: *SOMEONE'S COMING.*

Sure enough, I could hear a voice at the bottom of the stairs.

"If you'll all follow me this way, I'll show you our visual arts wing...."

It was Mr. Crawley. He was always giving tours of the school, which I hadn't even thought about—until now.

And now he was headed right for us. It was too far to try to get back to Mrs. Ling's room. The boys' bathroom was off-limits with Mr. McQuade in there. And trying to get up the stairs to the roof was way too risky.

I looked at Matty. Matty looked at me.

HIDE, he mouthed, and we scattered.

I did the first thing I could think of: I scrambled right up and into that big trash can. It wasn't easy, either, with that sculpture under my arm, not to mention that the whole can was on wheels. By the time I was pulling the lid over my head, I could just see the girls' bathroom door swinging closed behind Matty, and I thought—*much better idea*.

But it was too late to change my mind. All I could do now was sit there in the dark and pray that Mr. Crawley would be gone before Mr. McQuade ever came out of that bathroom.

And if you're thinking that was too much to hope for—you're right.

Obviously, I couldn't see anything from where I was, but it doesn't take a genius to figure out what happened next. I guess that garbage barrel must have rolled right in front of the bathroom door while I was climbing inside, and I guess Mr. McQuade must have come out a second later, because the next thing I felt was a hard *BUMP!* against the side of the can...

...right before the whole thing started zipping

across the floor…

…right before—

SLAM

CRASH!

rrroll

SPLAM!

SMASH!

    I don't know if you've ever been inside a plastic garbage can while it's rolling down half a flight of stairs, but believe me, it's not as fun as it sounds. (Even if it doesn't sound fun at all.)

    By the time I hit the first landing, it wasn't just

me and a bunch of used paper towels spilling out of that can either. It was also Zeke's sculpture, which had been bumped, rolled, slammed, crashed, and smashed back into the million separate pieces it started out as.

And that, ladies and gentlemen, boys and girls, is what you call blowing it, *big-time*. Because this wasn't just a case of art-napping anymore. No, sir.

Now it was art murder.

CHAPTER 43

EVERYTHING I DESERVED, AND THEN SOME

They kept me in the office that afternoon, all the way through sixth and seventh periods, until Mom could get there for my execution.

I mean, for a meeting with Mr. Crawley.

Actually, I guess I mean both.

There were also a lot of heavy stares, and shaking heads, and me being told to wait outside. By the time it was all over, my punishment was kind of like Zeke's sculpture. It came in a whole lot of parts.

First of all, I wasn't allowed to take Mrs. Ling's class for the rest of the year. I could still take drawing, painting, and everything else, but I'd have to make up half a year of sculpture in eighth grade—if they even let me get that far.

Second, I actually had to apologize right to Zeke McDonald's face. They even pulled him out of eighth period so I could do it in the office while Mom and Mr. Crawley watched. I just tried to get it over with as fast as possible and not throw up.

Just for the record, I know that what I did was messed up. If someone demolished my sculpture, even by accident, I'd want more than a little "I'm sorry" from them.

But at the same time, none of that took away everything Zeke had done to me, and we both knew it. Maybe he deserved an apology for the sculpture, but that doesn't mean he didn't also deserve to be dropped into the lion cage at the zoo with a couple of pork chops stapled to his butt.

Meanwhile, all I could do was sit there and take it while Mom and Mr. Crawley kept handing out the consequences.

The third part of my punishment was a three-day in-school suspension—one day for stealing the sculpture and two days for destroying it. I don't know whether that was more or less than I deserved, but it didn't matter, anyway. In sixth grade, I had a *one*-day suspension and practically died of boredom. The chances of surviving all the way to day three seemed kind of small.

And just in case you're wondering, Matty did the smart thing. He waited inside the girls' bathroom until the coast was clear. Then he snuck down to Mrs. Ling's room and put Kenny's palm tree away before anyone even knew it was gone. So, obviously, I didn't say anything about him, or even Kenny, because what was the point?

I just wish I'd been smart enough to get out of this myself. Or lucky enough. Or *whatever* enough.

But this is me we're talking about. Mr. None-of-the-Above himself.

And it wasn't over yet. In a way, the worst part was still to come.

CHAPTER 44

RAFE KHATCHADORIAN, WORST SON EVER

All the way home, from Cathedral until we were driving up Killarney Avenue, Mom didn't say one word to me.

Not one word.

I guess I was supposed to talk first, but I couldn't think of anything good to say. "I'm sorry" just doesn't cut it when you're in trouble for the third, fourth, fifth…or hundred and twenty-seventh time, like me. So I just sat there and tried not to freeze to death.

BRRR!

Finally, after Mom found a parking spot near the house and turned off the car, I couldn't stand it anymore.

"Mom, I'm really sorry," I said. "I really, really am." (See? Totally lame, but I had to say *something*.)

"Sorry for getting caught?" Mom said. "Or for taking that sculpture in the first place?"

"Both," I said, before I realized that the right answer was "Sorry for taking that sculpture in the first place."

Oops.

"I mean—"

"It's not just that I'm angry, Rafe," she said. "I'm also really disappointed. After everything that happened last year, I was hoping Cathedral could be a fresh start for you. I guess it hasn't worked out that way, has it?"

I shook my head. I was feeling worse about this by the second.

"Maybe I don't belong at Cathedral," I said. "That's what everyone else thinks."

"Everyone?" Mom said.

"All the best artists, anyway. Like Zeke McDonald and his friends."

Mom took a deep breath. "Rafe, look at me," she said, so I did. "Has it ever occurred to you that those other students might feel threatened by you?"

Now I wanted to laugh. "Threatened?"

"Trust me—you're not the only kid walking around Cathedral wondering if you're good enough. Art is a competitive world, even in middle school. But if this is the way you're going to deal with your fellow artists, then maybe you're right. Maybe you shouldn't be there."

"No!" I said right away. "I want to be in art school."

She smiled, just a tiny bit. "I thought so," she said, and for about a tenth of a second, it seemed like she was done being mad.

Wrong.

"So here's the deal," she told me. "You're grounded until further notice. You'll go to school, you'll come home, you'll do your homework. That's it. When Christmas break starts next week, you'll be staying home as well. You won't be going anywhere unless it's with me."

"Until further notice?" I said.

"That's right," Mom said.

In other words, she hadn't even decided how mad she was yet. This could go on anywhere from a couple of days...to infinity.

See, it wasn't just Zeke's sculpture that got broken that day. I'd also broken Mom's trust, and maybe for the last time. Because after this, I didn't think she'd ever trust me again.

I mean, would you?

CHAPTER 45

How Rafe Survived His In-School SUSPENSION

(Mostly Thanks to Me)

By Leo the Silent

TURN THE PAGE!

LAS VEGAS 5 miles

CHAPTER 46

THE NEXT-BEST THING

So if I told you that by Christmas break I was ready to jump back into Operation: Get a Life, would you think I was crazy? Stupid? Really, really forgetful? Let me explain.

The way I saw it, I had a kind of technicality on my hands. Technically, the mission was in a time-out when I got that suspension. So technically, I wasn't required to call GAME OVER.

In fact, the more I thought about it, the more it seemed obvious. Everything had been way better—not perfect, but better—right up until I called that time-out in the first place. That's when I started messing everything up.

It was time to get back to Getting a Life.

And of course, I didn't have to ask Leo twice. The conversation went something like this:

That just left the little complication of me being grounded (until further notice). We were going to have to figure out a way to come up with all new stuff without ever leaving Killarney Avenue.

But between me and Leo, I was pretty sure we could think of something. Like Mom always says— it just takes a little imagination. And if there's one thing both Leo and I have, it's that.

So let's just call this next part—

CHAPTER 47

HAPPY HOLIDAZE

I'm not saying all the stuff Leo and I came up with over break is going to put me in some kind of Hall of Fame for Awesomeness (or even Semi-Awesomeness), but we didn't do too badly. I guess you can judge for yourself.

Made my own Christmas cards!
(okay, just one for Jeanne Galletta and one for Ms. Donatello—but they were sorta cool.)

Merry Christmas!

POP-UP!

pull tab!

Jeanne

from Rafek

Learned how to make an apple pie from Mom. (Lots of extra cinnamon!)

Cleaned up a vacant lot with Mom, Georgia ...and a bunch of other people on Killarney Ave. (Extra credit for good deeds!)

Learned to fix a leaky toilet from Grandma (and believe me, we've got one).

Slept one whole night in the bathtub. (*Almost* as comfortable as that couch.)

I walk on your food!
HISSS   HISSS
Found a COCKROACH —yikes!— and put him outside. (I'm guessing he froze to death.)

Eight-hour Go Fish marathon with Georgia. (Won 38 out of 42 games. Georgia never remembers to cover up her cards.)

STARED AT A PENCIL FOR ONE SOLID HOUR. (I swear *it moved* ...just a little.)

For Christmas I wasn't exactly rolling in cash, so I gave coupons for anything that Mom, Grandma, and Georgia wanted me to draw. They all said themselves, and for part of the day I was like a real artist, drawing each of them as they sat for their portraits. They even got to pick where they wanted to be, and I drew that too.

It was also the first time I'd given my own art as a real gift, and I guess since it was Christmastime, Leo said I could count it as three things for the Get a Life list instead of just one.

Hey, I'll take it. Merry Christmas to me too!

CHAPTER 48

GO BIG OR GO HOME

By the end of Christmas break, my Get a Life list had 114 things on it. That meant 81 to go, with 77 days until the Spring Art Show at Cathedral. I was a little bit behind, but it wasn't too bad, seeing as I'd been chained to Grandma's house for the last two weeks.

And I must have been doing something right, because Mom said I could be not completely grounded once school started up again. I asked her what "not completely" meant, but she just said, "Let's see how it goes" and "Don't push your luck." I didn't ask any more questions after that.

Now that I was going to have a little more freedom, I knew exactly what I wanted to do with it. I'd been racking up plenty of small stuff over break, but it was time to start thinking big again.

Like really big.

Like Bigfoot Hairy big.

It had been a while now, and maybe if I was lucky, Hairy had taken an anger-management class or something. Anyway, I was determined to at least *try* to get him to tell me something about my dad.

But I wasn't going in without backup. I needed someone who already knew about the whole Dad situation and who didn't scare easily. Also, someone who was a real live human being. (Sorry, Leo!)

So as soon as I got to school on the first day back, I went looking for you-know-who.

I found him at his locker, drawing a new pair of eyeballs on the door to replace the ones Mr. McQuade had cleaned off over the break.

"Khatchy!" he said when he saw me. (He'd never called me that before, but that's Matty the Freak for you.) "What'd you get me for Christmas?"

"The other half of your brain," I said. "What'd you get me?"

Matty shrugged and unzipped his backpack.

Then he took out this sweet stainless-steel pen, still in the package.

"I'm not so big on wrapping stuff," he said, and tossed it at me.

Now I felt stupid. I hadn't even thought about getting a present for him. And the pen looked really nice, like something a real artist would use.

It also looked expensive.

"Um…how'd you get this?" I said, because with Matty, you never knew.

"Don't worry about it," he said. "I got some crazy money from my aunt this year."

I wasn't sure if he was telling the truth, but it's not like I was going to call him a liar right after he'd given me a present.

And right before I wanted to ask him a favor.

"So, listen," I said. "You remember Bigfoot Hairy, right?"

"I remember running for my life, if that's what you mean," Matty said.

"How would you feel about going back over there for a little surveillance with me?" I said.

I'd learned to speak enough Freak by now that I was pretty sure I knew how to get Matty interested. And sure enough, the way he smiled when I asked that question, you would have thought I'd just given *him* a present, not the other way around.

I think that's what you call a win-win situation.

CHAPTER 49

STAKEOUT!

Mom said I could hang out with Matty after school one day that week, as long as I was home by six o'clock. (I guess that's what not-completely-grounded meant.) In other words, we had to make this count.

One thing I knew for sure: If I was going to talk to Hairy, it wasn't going to be inside that barbershop, where there was only one exit. And all those scissors. So we set ourselves up in the building across the street, like a couple of real detectives on a stakeout.

Okay, it wasn't exactly like that. It was more like Matty calling the barbershop with a fake voice to find out what time Hairy closed, and then the two of us sitting at a bus stop on Calumet Avenue, waiting to see what would happen.

At ten to five, Hairy started sweeping up for the day. That's when I started getting a little nervous—and by a little, I mean I'm glad it was freezing cold out so I had an excuse for all that shivering.

By the time Hairy came out, wearing a black

biker jacket, I was literally shaking in my boots. But I wasn't going to quit now. Especially not in front of Matty.

"Let's go!" he said, and jumped right up.

"Hang on," I said.

I don't think Matty was used to following other people's plans, but I made him sit tight until Hairy got about halfway up the block. It wasn't hard keeping an eye on him either, since he was about twice as tall as anyone else around.

"Okay, now we can go," I said, and we started following Hairy.

At first, it was stop and go. We snuck up the street a little, then hid behind a newsstand. Then we went a little more, then stopped in the doorway of a shoe store.

"What are you going to say to him, anyway?" Matty asked me.

"I don't know," I said. "I'll figure it out if I have to."

"*If*?" Matty said. "What do you mean, *if*?"

"Shh!"

Hairy had just stopped in the middle of the sidewalk for no reason. I turned around fast and pulled down my hat, trying not to have a nervous breakdown right there.

"What's he doing?" I said. "Wait—don't look!"

"Relax," Matty said. "He's just tying his shoe."

We waited for Hairy to start moving again, then fell in behind.

He was going faster now, and it was getting harder to keep up. By the time Hairy turned the next corner, Matty and I were running to get there. We hoped we'd spot him on the next block, before he took another turn.

But there was something I wasn't counting on. Bigfoot Hairy was smarter than he looked. As soon as we poked our heads around that corner, he was right there waiting for us.

It was an ambush! He clamped one gigantic paw on the back of Matty's shirt, and another one on my arm.

"RUN!" Matty said, like there was any chance of that now.

Because Hairy wasn't just onto us. He *had* us. And I was pretty sure I'd just made the last stupid mistake of my life.

You know how they say your life flashes in front of your eyes when you think you're about to die? It's not true.

What I saw was a fifty-foot pile of hair, muscle, and tattoos flashing in front of my eyes.

"What the heck are you two dummies following me for?" Hairy said. (He didn't actually say "heck" or "dummies," but this is supposed to be a PG kind of book.)

"We weren't following you!" Matty shouted at him.

"DON'T LIE TO ME!" Hairy roared back, and held on even tighter. It felt like he was twisting my arm into some kind of balloon animal, and Matty's feet were practically off the ground.

The next part just kind of popped out of me. There wasn't any plan, except for trying not to die.

"You're my dad's uncle!" I yelled. (Okay, maybe kind of screamed, but in a really manly way.) "Hairy Khatchadorian, right?"

It was weird. Hairy didn't move a muscle. He just kind of froze. But there was about 75 percent less murder in his eyes.

Then he said, "Rafe?"

Let me tell you, I was not expecting that.

"How do you know my name?" I said.

"I can't believe this," he said. "I knew you when you were three years old. Heck, I knew you when you were born. I even changed your diaper a few times."

Matty laughed when Hairy said that, which made me kind of mad. But I had bigger things on my mind, and I didn't want to wait around for another one of the guy's mood swings. So I just kept going.

"Do you know where my dad is?" I asked him.

He let go of us and shoved his hands in his pockets, giving me a kind of funny look. For a second, I even thought he was about to answer my question.

But...no.

"Listen, Rafe," he said. "That's something you need to take up with your mom. Where is she, anyway?"

"She's home," I said, and he looked confused. "We live here in the city now."

"You do? But she always hated the city," he said.

"She did?" That was news to me.

"Come on, mister," Matty piped up. "He just wants to know about his dad. Why can't you—"

That's when the old Hairy came back.

"You mind your own business, kid," he said, but it also sounded a lot like "I could kill you with one punch, kid." I've never seen anyone stare Matty the Freak down so fast. (Or at all, actually.)

"Go home, Rafe," Hairy told me. "Talk to your mom first. Then if you want to, you can come back and see me. I've got some stories I could tell you about your old man."

I didn't know what to say to that. I didn't even know what to think. I just stood there like a statue with its mouth hanging open while Hairy patted me on the shoulder and started walking away up the street.

I even kind of forgot Matty was there until he spoke up again.

"Hey, check it out!"

When I looked down, there was a ten-dollar bill sticking out of my coat pocket.

"How'd he do that?" Matty asked.

"Beats me," I said while my mind just kept spinning around and around, like the inside of a washing machine.

I guess there were still a lot of things I didn't know.

CHAPTER 51

NOT RiGHT NOW

I got home with two minutes to spare before six o'clock.

When I came into the kitchen, Grandma was cooking dinner, Mom was painting on her little easel by the back door, and my head was still on the spin cycle. I couldn't stop thinking about the last thing Hairy said to me.

He had stories? About my dad? What kind of stories? How many?

"Well, look who it is," Dotty said. "My favorite grandson."

"Hey, Rafe-asaurus," Mom said. "Thanks for making it home on time."

I came over and she gave me a hug and kiss hello, which Mom always likes to do, even when she's working.

"What are you painting?" I asked her.

"It's a cityscape," she said. "The idea of one, anyway."

I can never tell what Mom's abstracts are supposed to be until she clues me in, but then I can almost always see what she's talking about. This one had a lot of straight lines going in all different directions. Kind of like city streets.

I could tell she was excited about it too. Mom hadn't sold a painting since we moved to the city, but she sure was trying.

"What do you think, mister art student?" she said. "Am I headed in the right direction?"

"Definitely," I said.

Mom just kind of smiled at that and went back to painting.

And even though my brain was still overflowing with everything that had happened that day, I decided right then that I wasn't going to talk about it after all.

Not yet, anyway. I'd just barely gotten ungrounded, and Mom was as happy as I'd seen her in a long time. Also, Dotty was making pancakes, and I *love* breakfast for dinner.

Why would I want to mess with all that?

So instead of having some big, uncomfortable conversation that night, we talked about painting instead. And drawing. And school. And the family of pigeons living on the roof across the street.

I didn't know when it was going to be a good time to start asking Mom all those Dad questions. I just knew that right now wasn't it. So for the time being, I was going to keep them to myself and my drawing pad.

(And to Leo, of course.)

CHAPTER 52

THiRTY-TWO TRiLLiON AND COUNTiNG

A few weeks into the quarter, Mrs. Ling came around to all the art classes and made an announcement.

"Boys and girls, it's that time of the year," she said. "Time to start thinking about your projects for the Spring Art Show."

But of course, I was already thinking about mine. I'd been thinking about it for months.

I'd never been in a real art show before, and I was going to make this the 195th thing on my list of 195 things. It was like the big finish line for Operation: Get a Life.

My project was going to be awesome!

Just as soon as I figured out what it was going to be.

"Remember," Mrs. Ling said, "this is your chance to really show us who you are as an artist, as well as the kind of artist you might become if you continue on here at Cathedral."

And that was a big part of my problem right there.

First of all, how was I supposed to show who I was "as an artist" when I didn't have the first clue?

And second—hello, pressure! The Spring Art Show was my last chance to prove I belonged in art school. I still didn't know whether I was going to make it back for eighth grade...or not.

In fact, it seemed like the more Mrs. Ling talked, the more problems I had.

"This is an open assignment," she told us. "That means you can work with any materials you like, to create anything you can think of."

That may not sound like a problem, but it was. See, it's one thing when they tell you to make a self-portrait, or a junk sculpture, or whatever. But when you can do *anything*, it's like getting a multiple-choice test with one question and thirty-two trillion possible answers. Good luck choosing the right one.

It didn't help that all the students but me seemed to already know what they wanted to do either.

"In the meantime," Mrs. Ling said, "to help you along, we have a lovely field trip to the Art Institute coming up. I hope you'll use that opportunity to take in some of the amazing art in this city and get inspired to reach new heights with your own work."

New heights? Who said anything about *new* heights? I was still working on reaching some old heights. Or any heights.

All of a sudden, that big finish line I'd been thinking about all year was starting to come up—*fast*.

CHAPTER 53

FIVE-DOLLAR POSTCARDS, SOME GUY NAMED MONDRIAN, AND A FEW OTHER THINGS THAT WENT OVER MY HEAD

By the time the Art Institute field trip rolled around, I'd had lots of time to think about my project for the Spring Art Show. And after some long, hard, careful consideration, I'd finally managed to come up with…zero good ideas.

But maybe Mrs. Ling was right. Maybe this field trip was going to inspire me to do something I'd never even thought about before. Maybe I'd get the best idea of my life here.

And if not…well, at least it got us out of a whole morning of regular classes.

When we got to the museum, they set us loose with our sketchbooks so we could walk around the galleries and draw whatever grabbed us. Matty seemed like he knew what he was doing, so I let him lead the way.

For a while I kept expecting him to pull something Matty-ish, like taking money from the fountain out front, or trying to get up on the roof, or at least touching some of the stuff you weren't supposed to touch in the museum.

But he didn't. As far as I could tell, he was actually interested in the art. We just walked around for a while and sketched some of the paintings, and then we walked around some more. It was a side of Matty I'd never seen before. He seemed so *normal*.

Which, for Matty, was so *weird*.

Finally, when Mrs. Ling came around and told us we had fifteen minutes left, Matty closed his sketchbook and started putting his stuff away.

"Come on," he said. "We don't want to miss the best part."

I followed him out to the front of the museum and then into the gift shop near the entrance.

"This is the best part?" I said.

"Trust me," he said. "Just check it out."

So I did, and let me tell you what I learned that day. Art museum gift shops are for rich people. Everything in that place cost about ten times more than you'd think. Even the postcards were five bucks each.

After a while, Matty came over to where I was.

"Hold this," he said, and gave me his backpack. "I have to go to the bathroom. But wait for me here, okay?"

I didn't really think about it. I just took his pack and kept looking at this hundred-dollar book about some guy named Mondrian, who got famous for painting a bunch of red, yellow, and blue squares, over and over. It made me think maybe I should get my own art book someday.

Who is this guy???

Just after that, though, I saw Mrs. Ling waving at me to come get on the bus. It was time to go.

I could see Matty too. He was still on his way to the bathroom, so I figured I'd give him his stuff outside.

But then, as soon as I started leaving—

The gift-shop alarm was going off, like someone had just walked out with something that wasn't paid for. And because I'm not always the swiftest boat on the water, I started looking around to see if I could figure out who the thief was.

And that's when I realized—the only person standing there was *me*.

SET DOWN THE BAG AND STEP AWAY!" the chief criminal negotiator screams into a bullhorn. It's almost impossible to hear, with the choppers so low and all those police sirens.

Something's gone very wrong here, and all I know is, I didn't do it.

"This is a mistake!" I yell.

"STEP AWAY FROM THE BAG! THIS IS YOUR FINAL WARNING!"

I hear footsteps—people are running everywhere. And shouting. Police radios are blaring. Is this really all for me?

I'm not taking any chances. I keep my hands where everyone can see them. Then I bend down slowly and set the pack on the ground.

As soon as I do, a dozen lines drop out of the sky. A football team's worth of SWAT officers rappel down to the ground all at once. Before I can even move, they've got me surrounded with enough hardware to...well, to open a really, really big hardware store.

"DON'T MOVE A FREAKIN' MUSCLE!" one of them shouts.

"PARDON ME, YOUNG MAN, BUT COULD YOU PLEASE STEP BACK INTO THE GIFT SHOP?" a third one says.

Wait-huh??????

CHAPTER 55

NOT IT

You can put your arms down, kid," the guard told me. "Just step back into the gift shop, please?"

Mrs. Ling was headed over by then. I could see Matty too. He was standing with the rest of the class now and looking right at me. But he wasn't coming any closer.

"Rafe?" Mrs. Ling said. "What's going on?"

"I don't know," I said. "But I didn't do it."

The guard asked her if he could check the backpack, and Mrs. Ling looked at me, like the choice was mine.

I just handed it over. He unzipped it right there on the gift-shop counter, and a second later he was pulling out one of those stainless-steel pens, still in the package. It was the exact same kind Matty had given me for Christmas, except mine was safe and sound at home.

"Rafe, can you explain this?" Mrs. Ling said.

I kept looking over at Matty, and he was just shaking his head—*no, no, no, no, no. Don't tell.* That's what he was saying. I felt like I was trapped, with my own head on the chopping block.

Except then, I started thinking—

You know how sometimes you can have a whole truckload of thoughts all at once? That's what happened to me. I remembered all those times I'd gotten into trouble that year—and all those times Matty had gotten away.

I'm not saying I blamed him. Most of it was probably my own fault. Or even *all* my fault.

But this time I hadn't done anything wrong. And I couldn't afford to pretend that I had.

"It's not my backpack," I said. "I didn't put that pen in there."

"Well, whose pack is it?" the guard said.

"I don't want to say," I told him.

"Then you're going to have to come with me."

"Rafe, answer the question," Mrs. Ling told me. "Whom does that pack belong to?"

My heart was bouncing around like a pinball, and I still wasn't exactly sure what to do. At least, not until I looked out into the lobby one more time. That's when I saw Mr. Crawley herding the whole rest of the seventh-grade class toward the exit. And you'll never guess who was right there in the middle of the crowd, trying to make a clean getaway and not even looking at me anymore.

Actually, you probably can guess.

"It's Matty Fleckman's," I said.

CHAPTER 56

MAD MATTY

I didn't get to find out what happened to Matty after that. All I knew was that he didn't ride the bus back to school, and neither did Mr. Crawley. And I guess he admitted to taking the pen—or maybe they even had it on a security camera—because I wasn't in trouble anymore.

That night, I tried tracking him down with everything but bloodhounds. I called him a bunch of times, but he never answered. I e-mailed him twice, but I didn't hear back. I even texted him from Mom's phone and said that it was about "homework," since Mom could see what I'd written, and I couldn't exactly say it was about "the pen you might or might not have tried to get me to steal for you."

That was the thing. I didn't know if Matty had

tried to set me up at the museum or if he really was going to come back and steal that pen for himself.

So I wasn't even sure if I was supposed to be mad at him, or if he was mad at me…or both…or neither…or *what*. In fact, it was driving me kind of crazy.

Finally, around nine o'clock, the phone rang. I ran into the kitchen to pick it up, but Grandma beat me to it.

"HELLO, AND WHAT'S SO IMPORTANT THAT SOMEONE HAS TO CALL MY HOUSE IN THE MIDDLE OF THE NIGHT?" she said.

No surprise, whoever it was hung up.

"Hmm," Grandma said. "I must have scared them off."

As soon as she left the room, I took the phone out on the back stoop and closed the door behind me. Then I dialed Matty's number.

I didn't really expect him to pick up—but then he did.

"What?" he said.

"Did you just call me?" I said.

"Oh, it's you," he said. "Hang on a second. Don't go away."

I heard him put down the phone. Then it was just quiet.

And then it stayed quiet for a long time. In fact, it probably took about three minutes before I finally figured out what was going on.

I guess that answered one question, anyway— about whether Matty was mad at me. And now that I knew, it made me think of something else. Something much scarier.

Let me put it this way: If I was going to count down the top five reasons why it was good to

have Matty the Freak for a friend, it might look
something like this:

(#5) He's really smart, even if he doesn't seem like it.

(#4) He's crazy like Leo, but real like me.

(#3) He's got a ton of good ideas.

(#2) He doesn't care what other people think.

And the number one reason
why it's good to have Matty
the Freak for a friend . . .

 **Believe me. You do NOT
want to have him for
an enemy.**

Watch your
BACK.

CHAPTER 57

THE FIRST PART OF THE WORST PART

Remember how I said earlier that Matty never did anything halfway?

That's what I was afraid of. I'm not going to say I was paranoid when I got to school the next day, but I did feel a little bit like I was being hunted.

It didn't take long to find out what was going to happen next either. The closer I got to my locker, the more I saw people in the hall looking at me and whispering to each other.

And here's what they were whispering about:

I guess the good news was that all the paint was on the outside this time. Any other day and I might have thought Zeke and Kenny had struck again.

But that "GET A LIFE" was like code. Matty was the only person at Cathedral who knew about Operation: Get a Life. And as far as I could tell, he was also the only person *not* standing around laughing at me right now.

So I went looking for him.

He wasn't hard to find. He always hung out on the back stairs before first period. When I got there, he didn't even look up, which only made me madder.

"What's your problem?" I said.

"You don't rat on a friend," he said. "That's what."

"Yeah, well, you don't let a friend get caught with something *you* stole," I said.

"I was coming back."

"How was I supposed to know that?"

"Because I *said* I was," Matty told me. Now he looked me right in the eye—and maybe he was telling the truth, and maybe he wasn't. I'd seen what a good liar he could be.

"Yeah, well, you've had your little fun," I said. "Now back off."

Matty closed his sketchbook and stood up. Then he got right in my face and gave me this familiar smile. I'd seen it before, and it always looked kind of evil and funny to me at the same time.

But right now it just looked evil.

"I'm not afraid to fight you, Matty," I told him.

"No," he said. "But you're so afraid of getting in trouble, you're not going to do anything about it, are you?"

I didn't answer—mostly because he was right.

This was the worst part. Matty knew me better than anyone else at school, and I'd told him way more than I ever should have. Now it was too late to take any of it back.

"And by the way," he said, "I'll let you know when I'm done having fun."

Then he just walked away while I stood there and watched.

I couldn't believe this was happening. A day earlier, we were supposedly friends. Now, as soon as he gets into a little trouble instead of me, we weren't friends anymore? As far as I was concerned, he was just being a big baby about the whole thing.

A big...

unpredictable...

highly dangerous...

baby.

CHAPTER 58

THE REST OF THE WORST

I spent the rest of the morning wondering what Matty's next move was going to be.

By fifth period, I was so tired of watching out, I was ready for a nap.

Of course, that wasn't going to happen. For one thing, I didn't want to give Matty a chance to tattoo my face or roll me out the window.

And for another thing…just because my day wasn't already complicated enough…we also had a crit that period.

This one was for a digital-art unit that Mr. Crawley had been teaching. The assignment was to take our own pictures and then cut them up on the computer and make a new image with them.

In fact, I actually liked my finished thing. I'd

gotten Matty to take a picture of me (back before we hated each other). Then I put parts of myself into another picture, of a brick wall, so it looked like someone had built the wall right up around me, with my arms, face, and legs sticking out in different places. I also made up my own graffiti on the computer and put that all over the wall too.

Not that I expected anyone else to like it. Zeke and Kenny basically had a rule about hating everything I did. And now I had to worry about what Matty was going to say too.

Or maybe he wouldn't say anything, because he'd be too busy figuring out how I was going to wind up under a bus after school. Either way, I wasn't looking forward to this.

The crits for digital art worked a little differently than the others. When you finished your assignment, you used your password to load it onto the school's computer. Then Mr. Crawley could pull it up and put it on the big screen at the front of the room for everyone to see.

And the reason I'm telling you this is because it was the one thing I didn't think about ahead of time.

Back when Matty and I were trying to get rid of

that fake RAFE K page of Zeke and Kenny's, I told him my password. It didn't seem like a big deal when I did it. I figured if there was one person at school I could trust, it was Matty.

And that might have been the biggest mistake I made all year.

"Okay, Rafe, let's see what you have for us," Mr. Crawley said when my turn came up. "What's the name of your piece?"

"*Kid in Wall*," I said. (What can I say? Titles just aren't my thing.)

Mr. Crawley punched a couple of keys on his laptop and pulled up my file. But instead of *Kid in Wall*, this is what came on the screen instead:

The whole computer lab went totally quiet. Nobody laughed. Nobody whispered. I don't even think anyone breathed.

At least, not for the first ten seconds or so.

After that, I couldn't tell you, because I'd already walked out of the room.

CHAPTER 59

I'M OUT OF HERE

The next thing that happened was something I'd thought about a million times in sixth grade but never actually did. I walked right out the front door of the school in the middle of the day and just kept walking.

I didn't care if I got in trouble. I didn't care if I got kicked out of Cathedral. I didn't care about any of it anymore. I just wanted one thing.

O-U-T.

"Where are we headed?" Leo asked.

"Home," I said.

"It's going to be suspicious if you show up too early," he said.

"Well, duh," I said.

Besides, I didn't mean Killarney Avenue.

I walked past my usual stop for the number 23 bus and kept going. Then I passed another bus stop, and another, and another. Nobody even looked twice at me, even though I was supposed to be in school. I guess that's one of the good things about living in a city.

It felt good to walk too. It gave me time to think—and to figure out exactly what my plan was going to be.

By the time I finally got all the way to Grandma's house, it was right around my usual time for getting back from school. That was good. I didn't want to draw too much attention to myself, in case I got stuck here for a little while.

Because as far as I was concerned, I was just passing through.

CHAPTER 60

JUST PASSING THROUGH

Hey, kiddo," Grandma said when I came in. "How was your day?"

"Um...unbelievable?" I said.

"That's nice."

"Is Mom around?" I asked. I hadn't seen her car out on the street.

"She went for another job interview," Grandma said. "But she'll be back."

Mom had been to so many interviews, it didn't really seem like it meant anything anymore. Nobody ever ended up giving her a job.

But it *was* going to make my next move easier.

As soon as Grandma went into the kitchen, I ran upstairs to Mom and Georgia's room. Georgia was on her bed, talking on the phone when I came in.

"Get out," I said.

"*You* get out," she said. "It's my roo—"

GET OUT!!!

I figured Georgia would run straight downstairs and cry to Grandma that I'd yelled at her. Or maybe stop along the way to mess with my stuff somehow. But I didn't care about any of that. I just needed to keep moving.

As soon as Georgia was gone, I opened Mom's

top dresser drawer and took out this little seashell-covered box she had in there. That's where she kept her "just in case" money. When I checked, there were three twenty-dollar bills folded up in a big paper clip.

I took two of the twenties and put one of them back in the clip, with a note.

The one other thing I took was Mom's key for the big storage locker in Hills Village where we still had a lot of our stuff—like my sleeping bag and some extra clothes.

Once that was done, I snuck halfway down the stairs and listened for Georgia's whining in the kitchen. I couldn't hear anything, but the coast seemed clear, so I kept going.

Then as soon as I got my hand on the front doorknob—

"What are you doing?"

I turned around and Georgia was right there, looking at me over the top of Grandma's big recliner. Seriously, she should get a job spying for the CIA. Like, in Mongolia would be nice.

"Nothing," I said. "But...tell Mom I'll call her later."

"Rafe?"

Georgia looked like she could tell something was up, and didn't want me to go.

"Sorry I yelled at you before," I told her. Then I opened the door and left before she could say anything else.

As soon as I hit the sidewalk, I started walking fast, back up Killarney Avenue the way I'd come just a few minutes before.

"Are you sure this is a good idea?" Leo said.

"No," I said. "But I'm going anyway. You coming?"

"Well, duh."

CHAPTER 61

ON THE ROAD AGAIN

CHAPTER 62

HEY, IF YOU HAD TO RIDE A HOT AND SMELLY BUS ALL THE WAY BACK TO HILLS VILLAGE, YOU'D START MAKING STUFF UP TOO

You okay, honey?" the lady next to me asked. "You seem like you're a million miles away."

"I'm okay," I said.

We were about halfway to Hills Village by now. It was too hot on the bus, and I was getting kind of sleepy.

"What's your name, sugar?" she said.

"Um…Leo," I told her.

"That's a nice name. Where are you headed, anyway?"

"I'm going to see my friend Matty," I said. "He's in

the hospital with this terrible flesh-eating disease."

The lady looked at me like she didn't know whether to believe me or not.

"He still owes me five dollars," I said. "So I need to get there before—well, you know. Before it's too late."

Now she was looking like maybe it was time for her to change seats.

"Just kidding," I said.

"Listen, Leo...aren't you a little young to be riding alone?" the lady asked me. She started reaching into her purse. "Is there someone I can call for you?"

"No, it's okay," I told her right away. "The truth is, I was just visiting my grandma in the city. My mom's going to pick me up at the bus station."

I looked her in the eye this time, but not too much—just right. Anyway, I think she bought it. She didn't ask any more questions, and the rest of the ride to Hills Village was quiet.

So I guess Matty the Freak taught me a thing or two after all.

Like how to lie.

CHAPTER 63

I'M BAAAAAACK!

It was REEEALLY weird getting off the bus in the middle of Hills Village.

There was the Duper Market, where Mom used to shop. There was the parking meter where I broke my tooth when I was ten. There was...some kid whose name I couldn't remember.

I felt like that Scrooge guy, who goes back to where he used to live and looks around without anyone knowing he's there.

"Hey, I'm the invisible one," Leo said. "If I were you, I wouldn't stick around downtown too long."

He was right about that. Hills Village isn't very big, and it was only a matter of time before I saw someone I didn't want to see.

I'd spent twenty-nine dollars on my bus ticket,

so that left eleven in my pocket. I used part of it for a bag of flaming barbeque chips and a can of Zoom at the FastMart by the bus station. Then I started walking again.

It was only about a mile to Jeanne Galletta's house, but by the time I got there, it was already dark.

(Yeah, that's right. *Jeanne Galletta's house.* Hey, I never said it was a good plan. It was just a plan.)

For a minute I thought about waiting until morning. But then I thought about everything I'd done to get there.

✓ Walk out of school
✓ Lie to Grandma
✓ Yell at Georgia
✓ Steal from Mom
✓ Take the bus all the way to H.V.

I wasn't going to stop now, just because it was night. So I walked right up the Gallettas' front walk and rang the bell.

Before anyone answered, one of the curtains in the front window was pulled back, and there was Jeanne. She looked like she couldn't believe what she was seeing.

Then the front door opened, and Mr. Galletta was standing right in front of me.

"Can I help you?" he said.

"Hi," I said. "Is Jeanne home?"

"Do you know what time it is, young man?" Mr. Galletta said.

I guess I could have been nervous. In fact, I probably *should* have been nervous. But you know when you see those people playing poker on TV, and they push all their chips into the middle of the table?

That was me right now. I was all in.

"Rafe?" Jeanne said. All of a sudden, she was there behind her dad. "Are you okay?"

"Hey, Jeanne," I said.

"Jeanne, what's going on here?" her dad asked.

"I don't know," she said. "What's going on, Rafe?"

"Not too much," I said. "I just wanted to come over and tell you…thanks for being so nice to me last year."

Now both of them were looking at me the same way that lady on the bus had—like I was definitely crazy, and maybe dangerous.

But I didn't care. I'd done what I came to do. At least I could say I finished *something* that year.

"Anyway, that's about it. I'll see you later, Jeanne," I said, and stepped off their porch.

Mr. Galletta was looking around the street now. "Are you alone?" he said.

"Yeah," I said. "I mean—not for long. My mom's just picking up some milk at the Duper Market. I'm supposed to meet her over there on the corner in a minute."

I could tell Jeanne didn't believe me, but before she could say anything, her dad was closing the door.

"Okay, then," he said. "Have a good night, Rafe. And not so late next time, okay?"

"Sure thing," I said, and started walking away.

I waited until I heard the Gallettas' door close before I looked back. When I did, Jeanne was at the window again, watching me. For some reason, that made me feel really good. I waved good-bye and then looked away quickly, before she could do it first.

But I didn't get very far. I was still on Jeanne's street when I heard Mr. Galletta again.

"Rafe?" he said.

I turned around, and he was coming after me. For a second I thought about running.

"Why don't you come back inside?" Mr. Galletta asked.

It wasn't really a question, though. And, besides, I just didn't feel like running anymore.

SLEEPOVER

O nce I was inside the Gallettas' house, they made me call Mom and let her know I was okay. She was pretty upset, but she didn't yell at me—not then, anyway.

Then Mrs. Galletta got on the phone and said a bunch of times that I "seemed fine" and that it was totally okay with them if I stayed there. After that, Mom said she was going to come get me first thing in the morning.

Let me tell you something: Of all the things I never, ever expected to happen in my life, I'd say that a sleepover at Jeanne Galletta's house was somewhere near the top of the list. Staying in their guest room that night was just about the weirdest possible ending to a *really* weird day.

Not that I slept much. Mostly, I just lay there and thought about Mom, and how stupid I was for doing this. Also, how glad I was thàt I didn't have to camp out in a dark, cold storage locker that night. (Seriously—what was I thinking?)

And when Mom said she was coming first thing in the morning, she meant it. By six o'clock, Mrs. Galletta was waking me up and asking Mom if we wanted breakfast before we left.

"We'll go out and get something," Mom told her. "I think we need to talk."

I was pretty sure that meant she needed to kill me in private, but I couldn't exactly say so. I just thanked Mrs. Galletta (Jeanne was still asleep) and walked out to the car.

As soon as we were alone, I started talking.

"Mom, I—"

But that was as far as I got. Mom leaned right across the seat and gave me this big, Grandma-size bear hug. She held on for a long time too.

"I'm sorry, Mom," I tried again. It didn't sound like much, since my face was mashed up against her coat, but I think she got it.

"Rafe, I'm the one who's sorry," she said.

"Mr. Crawley told me what happened at school yesterday, and I'm so, so sorry about that."

"You're not mad about me taking that money? And the bus?" I said.

Mom finally unhugged me and sat back. "Yes, of course I am," she said. "But there's something I need to tell you, Rafe. Something I should have already told you. What happened yesterday in your class only confirmed that for me."

"Mom, what are you talking about?" I said. There was something super serious going on, or I would have been in much bigger trouble by now.

Why wasn't she acting mad?

"I'm talking about your dad, sweetheart," she said. "I want to show you something."

CHAPTER 65

TRUTH

Did you already figure out we were going to a cemetery? Yeah, that's where my mom took me next.

And I can't say I was 100 percent surprised either. I just didn't know how much I already suspected until we were pulling up to the gate and I saw where we were.

Mom reached over and put her hand on top of mine. Not holding it, just more like covering it.

"Your dad was a soldier," she said. "He enlisted in the army when you were seven and Georgia was five. Then he went to war."

Mom looked at me, and her eyes were wet. I think maybe mine were too.

She took a box out of the backseat and showed

me a picture of Dad in his uniform, and a medal that I guess he got while he was overseas.

"Why didn't you say anything before?" I asked Mom. I didn't understand any of this yet.

"I'm sorry, Rafe," she said. "It's complicated for me. Your dad was a hero to his country, in the end. But he wasn't always a hero to our family. Not when he left us. It's been hard finding the right way to talk to you about this. But I absolutely should have."

I looked at that picture, and that medal, for a long time. Then I looked outside the car and around the cemetery.

"Where is he?" I said.

My mom pointed over toward some trees. "Over there, Rafe. Do you want to go and see?"

I took a really deep breath.

"Yeah," I said.

And that's what we did.

My mom took my hand, and we walked over to see my dad.

CHAPTER 66

TIME OUT

Okay, time out again.

I don't really know what to say about all this. I can't blame Mom for not telling me this stuff sooner. She was the one who'd been around all my life, not him.

It was sad and really strange finding out that my dad had died as a soldier, but at the same time, it didn't change much. Like I said before, I was used to everything the way it was.

In a way, the only thing that really changed was how I thought about my dad. Until then he was someone who'd run away and never come back.

But now he was a hero too.

I'm not saying that I wasn't sad about it and maybe a little confused. I'm just saying that I'm okay.

Okay?

So that's pretty much it. And just in case you're starting to think this book is going to have the world's saddest ending, let me tell you about everything that happened next.

It's actually pretty cool.

CHAPTER 67

TALL STACK

After we left the cemetery, Mom asked if I wanted to go get something to eat or if I just wanted to go home.

I know that in movies and stuff, people are always losing their appetites when something sad happens. But to tell you the truth, I was starving.

"Let's eat out," I said.

As we were driving back into town, we went by the place where Swifty's Diner used to be—and something amazing had happened.

Swifty's was back!

So of course, that's where we stopped and got breakfast. I ordered a tall stack with bacon *and* sausage, and Mom got a piece of Swifty's apple pie with a cup of coffee and orange juice.

When Swifty saw us, he came right out of the
kitchen. I'd never seen him and Mom hug before,
but they did then.

"Well, well, look who it is," Swifty said. "I thought
you'd left town."

Mom looked over at me and smiled. "We're just
back for a little visit," she said.

"That's too bad," he said.

"Too bad?" Mom said.

"I could really use you around here," Swifty

said. "Look—I even managed to save one of your paintings from the fire."

Sure enough, there it was on the wall behind the counter.

"Anyway," Swifty said, "you ever decide to move back to Hills Village, you let me know, Jules."

When he was gone, Mom sat back down in the booth across from me, and we were both looking at each other in this funny kind of way.

"Are you thinking what I'm thinking?" Mom said.

"I don't know," I said. "But I think I am."

We didn't even have to say it out loud.

Everything was about to change—again.

Because it always does, doesn't it?

MY HAPPY(iSH) ENDiNG

Boy, did things change!

I'm back in school now, finishing out the year at Airbrook Arts, where I was supposed to start seventh grade in the first place. Ms. Donatello went to bat for me—*again*—and they said I could do fourth quarter there, and then eighth grade after that, if I did some makeup work over the summer.

That's right. I'm going to be back in summer school, just like last year. Except this time it's because I want to be there. Crazy, right?

Of course, we're living back in Hills Village again—me, Georgia, Mom, and Grandma Dotty.

It turns out that even a semi-cruddy house in the city is worth something. Once we sold Grandma's, it was enough to help pay the rent on our new place for a long time. We're in an apartment now, not a house, but it's big enough for all four of us. That means no more sleeping on the couch!

I guess if there's a bad part to all this, it would be Matty the Freak. I tried calling him again before we moved out of the city, but he never called me back.

And you know what? That's okay too. I had a lot of fun with Matty for a while there, but I don't think he was ever a very good friend to begin with.

Besides, maybe none of this good stuff would have happened if he hadn't done what he did. So I can't be completely mad about that either. I even got to put him on my Get a Life list—twice! Not only did I make a friend for the first time in middle school, but I also lost one for the first time. (Hey, getting a life is all about the good *and* the bad, right?)

And yes, I still have my list. I'm up to 279 things now, and counting. Once I thought about it, I figured why stop at 195? Or ever? Sometimes Mom says life is just a work in progress, and that seems about right to me. I'm still working on getting a life, and MAYBE even turning myself into an artist. Who knows?

Which brings me to the last, very best thing that happened.

Swifty gave me something else I could add to my list that I'd never done before—my very own art show.

Maybe it was because the pressure was off...I don't know...but it didn't even take me long to figure out what I wanted to do. In fact, it kind of seemed obvious once I thought about it.

Turn the page and check it out.

RAFE K: LIFE IN PROGRESS

Everyone came to the opening reception at Swifty's and ate a ton of pie. Jeanne brought her parents. Ms. Donatello brought her husband. Bigfoot Hairy brought chocolate cigars. Even a couple of my new teachers at Airbrook were there. It was a little embarrassing, but in another way it was also kind of the best night of my life.

I mean…so far, anyway.

Hey, everyone, it's me—Rafe K. Thanks for reading my story. My next mission is already in the works, and it's CRAZY big. Stay tuned! Until then, I'm sending you to another middle school prison to meet another tortured middle schooler who really knows how to keep a kid laughing! Everyone is talking about Jamie Grimm. He's hilarious. So if you're looking for a story that's, well, even FUNNIER than mine, look no further. . . .

Chapter 1

FLOP SWEAT

THE PLANET'S
FUNNIEST
KID COMIC
CONTEST
NO LAME
Justin
Bieber
Jokes!
NO
adults
allowed!!
* * * * * *
NO
ONE REALLY
CARES WHY
THE CHICKEN
CROSSED THE
ROAD

Have you ever done something extremely stupid like, oh, I don't know, try to make a room filled with total strangers laugh until their sides hurt?

Totally dumb, right?

Well, that's why my humble story is going to start with some pretty yucky tension—plus a little heavy-duty drama (and, hopefully, a few funnies so we don't all go nuts).

Okay, so how, exactly, did I get into this mess—up onstage at a comedy club, baking like a bag of French fries under a hot spotlight that shows off my sweat stains (including one that sort of looks like Jabba the Hutt), with about a thousand beady eyeballs drilling into me?

A very good question that you ask.

To tell you the truth, it's one *I'm* asking, too!

What am I, Jamie Grimm, doing here trying to win something called the Planet's Funniest Kid Comic Contest?

What was I thinking?

But wait. Hold on. It gets even worse.

While the whole audience stares and waits for me to say something (anything) funny, I'm up here choking.

That's right—my mind is a *total and complete blank.*

And I just said, "No, I'm Jamie Grimm."

That's the punch line. The *end* of a joke.

All it needs is whatever comes *before* the punch line. You know—all the stuff *I can't remember*.

So I sweat some more. The audience stares some more.

I don't think this is how a comedy act is supposed to go. I'm pretty sure *jokes* are usually involved. And people laughing.

"Um, hi." I finally squeak out a few words. "The other day at school, we had this substitute teacher.

Very tough. Sort of like Mrs. Darth Vader. Had the heavy breathing, the deep voice. During roll call, she said, 'Are you chewing gum, young man?' And I said, 'No, I'm Jamie Grimm.'"

I wait (for what seems like hours) and, yes, the audience kind of chuckles. It's not a huge laugh, but it's a start.

Okay. *Phew.* I can tell a joke. All is not lost. Yet. But hold on for a sec. We need to talk about something else. A major twist to my tale.

"A major twist?" you say. "Already?"

Yep. And, trust me, you weren't expecting this one.

To be totally honest, neither was I.

Chapter 2

LADIES AND GENTLEMEN...ME!

Hi.

Presenting me. Jamie Grimm. The sit-down comic.

So, can you deal with this? Some people can. Some can't. Sometimes even *I* can't deal with it (like just about every morning, when I wake up and look at myself in the mirror).

But you know what they say: "If life gives you lemons, learn how to juggle."

Or, even better, learn how to make people laugh.

So that's what I decided to do.

Seriously. I tried to teach myself how to be funny. I did a whole bunch of homework and read every joke book and joke website I could find, just so I could become a comedian and make people laugh.

I guess you could say I'm obsessed with being a stand-up comic—even though I don't exactly fit the job description.

But unlike a lot of homework (algebra, you know I'm talking about *you*), this was fun.

I got to study all the greats: Jon Stewart, Jerry Seinfeld, Kevin James, Ellen DeGeneres, Chris Rock, Steven Wright, Joan Rivers, George Carlin.

I also filled dozens of notebooks with jokes I made up myself—like my second one-liner at the comedy contest.

"Wow, what a crowd," I say, surveying the audience. "Standing room only. Good thing I brought my own chair."

It takes a second, but they laugh—right after I let them know it's okay, because *I'm* smiling, too.

This second laugh? Well, it's definitely bigger than that first chuckle. Who knows—maybe I actually have a shot at winning this thing.

So now I'm not only nervous, I'm *pumped*!

I really, really, *really* (and I mean really) want to take my best shot at becoming the Planet's Funniest Kid Comic.

Because, in a lot of ways, my whole life has been leading up to this one sweet (if sweaty) moment in the spotlight!

Chapter 3

WELCOME TO MY WORLD

But, hey, I think we're getting ahead of ourselves.

We should probably go back to the beginning—or at least *a* beginning.

So let's check out a typical day in my ordinary, humdrum life in Long Beach, a suburb of New York City—back before my very strange appearance at the Ronkonkoma Comedy Club.

Here's me, just an average kid on an average day in my average house as I open our average door and head off to an average below-average school.

Zombies are *everywhere*.

Well, that's what I see. You might call 'em "ordinary people." To me, these scary people stumbling down the sidewalks are the living dead!

A pack of brain-numb freaks who crawl out of the ground every morning and shuffle off to work. They're waving at me, grunting "Hul-lo, Ja-mie!" I wave and grunt back.

So what streets do my freaky zombie friends like best? The dead ends, of course.

Fortunately, my neighbors move extremely slowly (lots of foot-dragging and Frankenstein-style lurching). So I never really have to worry about them running me down to scoop out my brains like I'm their personal pudding cup.

There's this one zombie I see almost every morning. He's usually dribbling his coffee and eating a doughnut.

"Do zombies eat doughnuts with their fingers?" you might ask.

No. They usually eat their fingers separately.

The school crossing guard? She can stop traffic just by holding up her hand. With her other hand.

Are there *really* zombies on my way to school every morning?

Of course there are! But only inside my head. Only in my wild imagination. I guess you could say I try to see the funny side of any situation. You should try it sometime. It makes life a lot more interesting.

So how did I end up here in this zombified suburb not too far from New York City?

Well, *that*, my friends, is a very interesting story....

Chapter 7

A STRANGER IN AN EVEN STRANGER LAND

I moved to Long Beach on Long Island only a couple months ago from a small town out in the country. I guess you could say I'm a hick straight from the sticks.

To make my long story a little shorter, Long Beach isn't my home, and I don't think it ever will be. Have you ever felt like you don't fit in? That you don't belong where you are but you're sort of stuck there? Well, that's exactly how I feel each and every day since I moved to Long Beach.

Moving to a brand-new town also means I have to face a brand-new bunch of kids, and bullies, at my brand-new school.

Now, like all the other schools I've ever attended, the hallways of Long Beach Middle School are plastered with all sorts of NO BULLYING posters. There's only one problem: Bullies, it turns out, don't read too much. I guess reading really isn't a job requirement in the high-paying fields of name-calling, nose-punching, and atomic-wedgie-yanking.

You want to know the secret to not getting beat up at school?

Well, I don't really have scientific proof or anything, but, in my experience, comedy works. Most of the time, anyway.

That's right: Never underestimate the power of a good laugh. It can stop some of the fiercest middle-school monsters.

For instance, if you hit your local bully with a pretty good joke, he or she might be too busy laughing to hit you back. It's true: Punch lines can actually beat punches because it's pretty hard for a bully to give you a triple nipple cripple if he's doubled over, holding his sides, and laughing his head off.

So every morning, before heading off to school, just make sure you pack some good jokes along with your lunch. For instance, you could distract your bully with a one-liner from one of my all-time favorite stand-up comics, Steven Wright: "Do you think that when they asked George Washington for ID, he just whipped out a quarter?"

If that doesn't work, go with some surefire Homer Simpson: "Operator! Give me the number for 911!"

All I'm saying is that laughing is healthy. A lot healthier than getting socked in the stomach. Especially if you had a big breakfast.

Read more in

I FUNNY

Coming December 10, 2012!